Orange Dawn

John Clark Smith

Setu Publications
PITTSBURGH, USA

Orange Dawn
A Novella
By

John Clark Smith

Setu Publications
* Pittsburgh, PA (USA) *

We would be pleased to receive email correspondence regarding this publication or related topics at setuedit@gmail.com.

ISBN-13 (paperback): 978-1-947403-07-9
Cover Designer: Rachel Power
Printed and bound in the United States of America.
Distributed to the book trade worldwide by Setu Publications, Pittsburgh (USA)

Setu Literary Publications, Pittsburgh, USA

Orange Dawn

By

John Clark Smith

DEDICATION

To all the workers throughout the world who are trying to save our environment and protect our flora and fauna.

Orange Dawn

By

John Clark Smith

Acknowledgements

Special thanks to Alissa York, novelist and Professor at Humber College, for her careful criticism and suggestions on every page of this novella. The final work is, of course, my responsibility. As always, thanks to my wife Susan, who not only reads and improves all of my work but has always been a great support. Finally, a note of appreciation to Anurag Sharma at Setu Publications for his help in bringing the book to print.

ORANGE DAWN

Table of Contents

Preface

The mountains, valleys, forests, rivers and lakes of Western Pennsylvania are filled with a treasure trove of plant and animal life. I have often traveled and stayed there, have walked and camped in its woods, eaten at its restaurants, spent hours staring at the beauty of its environment, all the while sharing time with my family. It's an inspirational environment and perfect as a setting for this story.

Yet Western Pennsylvania is not alone in having this wonderful diversity. The earth is still filled with similar places, and this story could happen in any of them.

Today, while the beauty remains, it's a fragile beauty in danger of slowly disappearing. This story is a testament to the diverse beauty of life. To modify John Donne's famous statement in *Meditation* XVII, any flower's death diminishes me because I am involved in the life of every living thing. Should we lose that connection, we die, since we are all interrelated and depend upon the other.

Rachel Carson, who wrote *Silent Spring* and *The Sea Around Us*, said in a speech that "the more clearly we can focus our attention on the wonders and realities of the universe about us, the less taste we shall have for destruction."

I humbly hope this novel will have a similar effect, that we will believe, after finishing it, that we must find ways to safeguard our living world and end our need for destruction.

John Clark Smith

Chapter 1

Even after many years I can summon that powerful evergreen scent from tne Allegheny Mountains in western Pennsylvania. It arose from woods so thick that I could rarely see more than a few feet into them. The rusted oil pumps, like monstrous metal grasshoppers, would appear occasionally. Once squeaking away without rest, the pumps were reminders of a generation that believed it had unending resources. To a future race they might be thought the relics of a religion, like the giant stone figures of Easter Island.

I had been driving on Route 6 and had missed a turn. I could've turned around, but the dense woods were calming – so calming I was unaware I was going in circles. Eventually I realized I had to ask for directions. I noticed a hut set far back off the road with smoke streaming from its chimney.

After parking the car, I made my way through a thick section of red maples and elms past two pumps. I heard finches and sparrows in the trees and chipmunks moving upon the dry pine needles and dead branches. A smell made me gag before I came to a wide stream. On the surface dead insects floated in patches of scum. Otherwise it appeared clear, though there was nothing visibly living in it. I covered my nose and mouth. How could the stench that belonged in a city sewer appear here in such a gorgeous forest?

I placed a large tree branch over the stream, crossed and hurried on. Away from the stream, the area smelled like home. When I was a girl, we had often travelled through the Alleghenies on our way to my grandparents' house. I would press my nose up against the partially open backseat window, mesmerized by the unending forests. Deep in those woods, on one of my many hikes with my Dad, I saw a little head peeking from behind a tree. Panting heavily, the stray was barely more than a bunch of fur on a skeleton. He became Rusty, my first dog. As an adult, I had often camped nearby, memories calling me to return.

The hut appeared to be a one-room wooden structure set on cement blocks in a well-groomed clearing. Piled under the structure were carefully cut mirrors of the same size. I looked down into one of them and saw me, a woman surrounded by massive firs questioning if she should return to her car,

I surveyed the environs like a wary animal and approached the door. My hope was that the one inside would be friendly. I finally knocked, still prepared to run back to my car. No one answered, though I could hear movement within. I walked around the back and noticed a path leading into the forest. Down the far end, there was an entrancing, bright orange light.

I looked back at the hut. No one appeared.

I proceeded slowly on the path, cautiously advancing toward the glow, occasionally glancing behind me. The glare increased on each step toward the clearing, coloring more and more of the trees along the way. I was entering an orange tunnel, its pulsating richness luring not only my eyes but also my mind. The light hypnotized me, as if there were small suns buried within it. Emerging into a clearing, I was almost blinded by the vortex of swirling light. I covered my eyes with my hands, then peeked through them. What could produce such an odd color, without smell or heat? The movement within it was dizzying.

When my eyes adjusted, I was overlooking a valley ringed by mountains. Below, I recognized the small city of Harding caught in the center of this inexplicable glow. The shade was brighter than the fruit, almost phosphorescent, with more yellow in it, as well as a kind of beguiling movement. It was impossible to gaze at it for long without briefly seeing spots.

I sat down to clear my eyes and marvel at the sight. The trees, grass, bushes and flowers seemed unaffected.

A loud voice jarred me. "Who are you?"

I turned. A tall, thin man stood before me in a black shirt and khaki pants. He had broad shoulders, long black hair and a few streaks of gray at the temples.

"I'm lost," I said.

He said nothing, watching me through bloodshot eyes with deep wrinkles at the corners.

"Well, not completely lost. My grandparents lived nearby."

"When were you here last?"

"Couple years ago."

He held out his hand. "I'm Paul Sheffield. I saw you from the hut."

His appearance coming up behind me along with the orange made me hesitate. But I stood up, shook his hand and introduced myself.

"This is no place to be lost," Paul said.

"Why?"

"Did you see the stream?" he asked.

"Yes. How did it happen?"

"You don't know? Of course, you don't." There was something almost entertaining about Paul—he swept his arms around as if he was gesturing to thousands. "Perhaps you'd like to learn more? It's not too long a walk to town. Time for me to go back anyway."

His invitation excited the kid in me, as if someone was daring me to cross a rickety bridge. It's only an orange light, I told myself. I had seen similar clouds of gray or yellow over cities or around heavy industries.

After all, no one was waiting for me, I thought, I had no schedule to keep. Paul seemed harmless. The orange is captivating. Why not take a little trip to Harding?

"OK, let's go."

*

As we came closer to Harding, with the orange ring hovering around us, I had a growing feeling of dread, as if that kid in me had lost her mother in the darkness. I hoped I wasn't stepping into another Chernobyl. Who could forget that twentieth-century newspaper headline in London that quoted what the Health officials had told nuclear workers: "Don't have babies!"

Though anxious, I couldn't resist the lure of the orange. It was as if I was standing on the edge of Niagara Falls and I yearned to jump in and become a part of it. I gazed in awe, as if it was calling to me.

Paul stopped, and looked down upon the town in a fixed stare. Finally, he moved away from the mountain path and sat on a boulder. "I'm not sure I should return."

We sat in silence.

"Yes, I should go," he said, convincing himself.

"What's stopping you?"

"My brother Ben, he's the Mayor, you know. He won't let anyone in or out."

"How can he stop you? You could sneak in—"

"He called the National Guard. They've put up roadblocks and are even patrolling the forest."

He looked at me.

"I hated to leave my friends, but they wanted me to go. We had a plan."

"But why did you leave?"

"You think such a light is normal?"

"Of course not."

"People are sick. Look at my hands, my hair. It changes people."

He shook his head in frustration.

"If I go back to Harding, perhaps I won't want to leave."

We sat beside each other on the boulder for some time, not speaking.

"You return to the hut," I finally said. The strangeness of it all had seduced me. "I'll go on."

He composed himself.

"No, no. I'll go too. Don't worry. Glen showed me a way."

"Glen?" I asked.

"Glen Harding. Knows this land better than anyone."

Excitement soon replaced apprehension as we continued down the slope. How extraordinary a single color could appear! Once I adapted to its brilliance, it had the soft feel of sunset in the way it colored the landscape, buildings and the metal grasshoppers. A tender and ethereal orange moonlight of the day.

But this impression wouldn't last. Beauty, I would soon learn, does not imply innocence.

Chapter 2

We slowly moved down the mountain to a cave entrance well-concealed behind a large rock and several large branches. The cave led to a tunnel which ended near where we would meet with Paul's friends on the western side of Harding.

The cave was only a brief journey. Most of our trip was through the dirt-lined tunnel. Despite Paul's flashlight, it was so dark that it was necessary for us to put our hands out to feel the walls. Often my hand would touch worms and insects. Occasionally streaks of light would appear—openings to the outside—and then we would fall to blackness again.

"The natives made these tunnels," Paul told me as we walked, hunched over. "There are many around Harding."

"Why?" I asked.

"Glen claims they were used in their Indian wars between the Iroquois and the Erie."

Occasionally we would feel or hear various creatures scurrying in and out of holes or on the floor of the tunnel. I assumed they were rodents, moles, or other animals. Several streams leaked into the tunnel and created their own brook. I wished I had brought along some rubber boots.

When we came to the end of the tunnel, the air still smelled as fresh as it had been on the mountain, though it seemed to be becoming increasingly difficult to breathe. My eyes were watering so badly I had to wipe them with a cloth.

"Where we headed?" I asked.

"Abe Fisher's."

"And who's he?"

"Someone I trust." He paused. "We started a journal together."

Near the bottom of the mountain was a tributary of the Allegheny River. The same signs of toxins that I had seen near the hut were visible in the water.

"How long has the water been like this?"

"Years," he said. "I remember when I was a kid, my parents telling me not to drink from the tributaries."

We jumped over a narrow section of the stream and entered a swampy area filled with dead branches, tall weeds and other flora in a constant state of death and rebirth. Though uninhabitable for humans, Paul said it was a haven for deer, bear, birds and other wildlife.

After the swamp there was a small forest of very old trees whose ground was composed of layers of pine needles. Once we passed through it, we were in sight of Harding.

"Look," he said.

In the distance I could see the backs of two National Guards standing at the end of a broad boulevard.

Despite my watery eyes and breathing problems, the pervasive tint was strangely relaxing. We were walking near an abandoned farmhouse when I asked him if I could rest, but I actually wanted to absorb the feeling. I sat on one of the rusty swings beside the house and swung back and forth, letting the marvelous orange swallow me in its radiance. He became impatient after a couple of minutes and we moved on.

"What's the journal about?" I asked.

"An alternative view of life in a small city."

"Sounds interesting."

"Not to my brother, especially when we talk about recent history. Glen has thoroughly researched that history and created a chronicle of the town. Then there's Tosh Jones, who's lived a lot of the history. He and my grandfather didn't get along. Abe and I edit and contribute essays. And of course, Melinda. She brings the feminist point of view. So, we've lots of material and some of its... well... not so kind to my family or some of the other citizens of Harding."

In front of Abe's apartment building were two pump-grasshoppers. I petted one of them as I passed. Abe greeted us at the door. His bright red cheeks, bald forehead, and clump of red hair sitting proudly at the back of his head, created a jolly impression, despite his tired eyes.

We followed him up the stairs and sat in the kitchen. Out the window, there was a view of the orange and surrounding mountains.

In one corner sat a mongrel puppy with mournful eyes. I tried to catch his interest, but he was apparently too weak to move. I rolled a ball before his nose. He just watched it go by. Bowls of uneaten food and water were beside him.

"Hey, Peirce." Abe sat down beside him on the floor. "C'mon, boy. Eat something."

He petted the dog's head and scratched his back.

"What's wrong with him?" I asked.

"Ever since the orange, he just lays there, looking up at me." He glared at Paul. "We might as well have sent Peirce."

They began to argue. Apparently, Paul was supposed to go to the next town and find a place for the group. Melinda especially wanted to get her daughter Aphra out. Very few children remained.

As the men bickered on, evening came through the window—an astonishing sight. I ran from the apartment building and stood looking at the spectacle. The translucent orange seemed to magnify light from the moon and the stars, as if they were on top of me. The sky was a distant black background behind the orange glow. Especially impressive was the way it painted the water and the metal grasshoppers.

Years ago such a sight might have been viewed as a divine visitation, but that mindset was long gone in most people. Such events were usually signs of real dangers, such as the noxious swamp near the rubber factory, an ice storm in Florida, or the transformation of a once living lake into a dead pond or a desert.

I would have remained longer, but after a few minutes I had to escape back into the kitchen from a coughing fit.

The view from the window kept me spellbound.

Paul brought me a glass of cold water, fresh and odorless.

As I stared out the window and brought the glass to my lips, an alarm went off in my mind. The stream's water had also been clear. But thirst prevailed and I drank.

I ran to the sink and spat it out. "The water is rancid!"

Paul and Abe looked at each other.

"You're imagining things," Paul said.

Abe waved Paul away. "The orange affects everyone differently."

Paul handed me a bottle of spring water. "I suppose it's as likely as any other reaction."

"But the air too?" I asked.

"What about it?" Paul said.

I threw up my hands. Perhaps my reactions happened because I was new. Perhaps the residents over time became immune.

Other events still puzzled me. What were the National Guard forces doing here? Why were people not leaving if they felt danger? And the orange, what exactly was it? I needed to roam about Harding and see how others responded to the orange. I fancied myself as the only one who saw the situation with an open mind, like a crusading lawyer coming to town to solve the case. It should have dawned on me that an open mind is only open to what it can understand.

Chapter 3

After spending the night on Abe's couch, I woke to the screeching blare of sirens. I covered my ears with cushions and waited for the attack on my nerves to end.

Moments later I felt a hand on my shoulder. Abe and Paul were looking down on me.

"What is it?" I shouted.

"Let's go!" Paul shouted back. "We need to go down to the square."

I pointed to the clock. "It's only six-fifty."

"We have to go."

My first thought involved food. Breakfast and coffee were on my mind. Yet if the air and water were unpalatable, would the food be any different?

As I sat up on the couch, a young woman and a girl walked in the room, the pair of them holding hands. The woman wore her blond hair in a tight ponytail. She was tall and slim with striking green eyes. The girl was a smaller version, clearly the woman's daughter. In the girl's arm was a stuffed animal, a snowshoe hare.

Paul introduced them as Melinda and her daughter Aphra.

"And why are you here?" Melinda asked, in a cold tone.

"She was lost," Paul answered for me. "I met her at the hut."

"And you thought it was a good idea to bring—"

"Hey, I warned her."

Melinda looked as if an idea had suddenly occurred to her. She gestured to Paul and Abe to meet her in the corner, where they began whispering.

While they conferred, I went to the washroom, swished some available mouthwash in my mouth, and cleaned my face and hands.

Looking up from the towel, I was surprised to find Aphra had followed me.

"You're not from Harding?" she asked.

"Nope. But I've traveled and camped around here a lot. My grandparents lived nearby."

"So you like the outdoors?"

"I do," I said, combing my hair. "I was a girl scout and my Dad was a survivalist. If he could, he would have lived in the woods."

"I think you're brave," she said, hugging her stuffed hare close. "You saw the orange and wanted to come. Things are going to happen here."

"They are?" I asked.

"You should leave. Take Peirce."

I smiled and walked back into the kitchen. "I don't think Peirce wants to come with me."

"I could tell you how, if you wanted to leave."

"You could?"

"Yep, I know all the tunnels."

"Well, if I need your help, Aphra, I'll let you know. Thanks."

"You're welcome."

In a few minutes the five of us were outside. Paul and Abe lived at the end of a boulevard. Beyond the boulevard was an unpaved gravel road on which there were a few farms before the mountains. The boulevard, once a section of a railroad track, led into town across a bridge.

The orange was as persistent as ever, and the air was still uncomfortable for me to breathe. I used a napkin to cover my nose and mouth to filter some of the effect, but I continued to have coughing fits. The sirens ended soon after we left and were replaced with a sweet bell that sounded every thirty seconds.

Paul kept up a good pace, as did the crowds of people heading downtown from different parts of the city.

"What's going on?" I asked. "Where're we going?"

"We're reporting," Paul said. "The sirens remind us. Our reporting station is in the town square."

"Is all this necessary?" I asked.

"Ha!" Paul laughed. "If you live here, it is."

"You see," Abe said, "when the orange came over a year ago, people were afraid to leave their houses. Absenteeism was epidemic. Businesses were struggling. People got fired or took all their sick days. It made no difference. Even the people in the government were hesitant to come to work. The town was dying.

So Ben Jr.—supported, by the way, by the state and federal governments—responded by making sure citizens went to work. Of course, it also allowed Ben Jr. to complete several projects."

"They also brought in the National Guard to make sure we behaved," Melinda said, pointing to the Guardsmen posted at the end of the boulevard.

Streams of birch trees lined the boulevard toward town. The white bark washed over with orange created an idyllic look, as if we were entering another realm.

"At the start," said Paul, "few citizens questioned Ben's ambitions and the need for the Guard. He convinced them that work was the only way to improve Harding and stop the orange.

"'We must not question!' Ben Jr. said. 'A special government research team has proven the orange is harmless and will eventually dissipate. Occupy yourselves. Focus on your city.'"

"The National Guard issued identity cards," Melinda said. "The town was locked down so no one could leave. Basically it's as if we've got the plague here and we're quarantined."

"They won't admit it, but they're worried about the orange spreading," Abe said.

"But what about Paul?" I asked. "He left."

"I swiped his card and told the check-in person he was sick," Abe answered. "They'll allow that, as long as they know the person and it's temporary. If he didn't return, then they'd punish me. We hoped we'd all be gone by then."

We passed a large plaque on a concrete pillar. I stopped to read it while the others continued. It commemorated the Härjedalen

(Harding) family as the first European settlers in northwestern Pennsylvania, and one of the rare European families who had contact with the Erie tribe.

I caught up with the group and asked them about the family.

Paul pointed to another marker close to the bridge. "That's where their cabin stood."

The uniquely carved configurations of rocks where the cabin stood were monuments to their children who died.

"I wish Glen was here," Melinda said. "He could give you a full history."

"I can do it," Aphra said.

"OK, go ahead," Melinda said.

"Well, when the Hardings came, the Erie tribe was still thriving, before their war with the Iroquois in the seventeenth century. The Hardings had a good relationship with the tribe. Several Hardings married native peoples. Others developed friendships. They were influenced by the native beliefs, especially in protecting the flora and fauna. For them injuring nature could offend the Great Spirit. Glen still wears the badge that refers to the panther, an important symbol in Erie cosmology. I do too."

Aphra showed me the badge that hung around her neck.

"The Erie leadership, like the Iroquois, was...I forget the word."

"Matrilineal," Melinda said.

"...matrilineal with veto power. They advised the chief to give land to the Härjedalen family that includes much of the city of

Harding. In exchange, the Härjedalens promised the tribe to protect the land and its wildlife. It's called the Harding Promise."

"Except," Abe said, "the Hardings couldn't uphold it. Governments and industry found ways to thwart them."

"Especially the Sheffields," Aphra muttered. "Not you, Paul."

"No, you're right," Paul said. "My grandfather encouraged industry that destroyed a lot of flora and fauna. And my brother's no different."

As I walked toward the bridge, transfixed by the orange glow on the river, I imagined a wonderful sunset when the Härjedalens would join their native friends at the river's edge. Together they would make music and dance, the European children playing with and learning from the native children. The natives would talk of the ancient days upon the land, when the spirits were everywhere. In turn, the Härjedalens would tell the folk tales of their homeland in Sweden.

We had passed several intersections, the last one following the path of the river. Now we stood before a truss bridge, originally used by the railroad but converted to a single-lane road and pedestrian path.

A large arch claimed that I was now entering the real Harding— even though the Härjedalen family lived beyond the arch. The others waited as I stopped to read the welcome sign that hung from the arch – the date of settlement and some of the prominent settlers.

On the other side of the bridge a park lay between us and the downtown. There were benches – some of them painted and quite attractive – more pumps, and boat launches, though there were no boats in sight. Brick streets went down to the river and to the square, and there was also a path along the river. The backs of restored buildings lined the riverbank, and parts of two old mills extended out over the river.

As we passed by several National Guardsmen, the crowd spread out within the park to form a haphazard group of lines. The space was insufficient to accommodate such numbers. The grass was worn to dirt in many places from these daily pilgrimages, the benches along the streets had been removed, the wading pool for children was covered, and a fountain with a statue of a child skipping rope in the middle was dry.

Standing in the Park were two dormant oil grasshoppers. Both of them were in beautifully restored condition and plated in gold.

"Is that real gold?" I asked.

Paul nodded. "The plaques list names of rich donors to Ben Jr.'s campaign, as well as businesspeople. There are plans for many others. Ben wants the money to build a stadium and sports arena."

We traversed the park to Main Street, already congested with a crowd walking north. As we joined the mass of human forms, no one spoke, the only sounds were countless soles smacking the road. Thankfully, the city square was a short distance from the Park. Bounded on all sides by restored buildings, it gave some breathing room. Still, no one could move far without being touched.

"Glen works there at the City Cafe," Melinda said, "on the west side, next to the original post office, and the convenience store."

"That's the courthouse," Paul said, pointing to the east side.

"Where Glen's grandfather took the State to court to defend the Promise," Aphra said.

"It's the oldest building remaining in Harding," Abe said. "Well, there's the jail too."

"But the most remarkable feature," Melinda said proudly, "are the second-floor balconies See, they're linked by bridges over the roads and sidewalks so that it's possible to walk all the way around."

"Quite unique," I said.

"Who's that statue in the middle of the square, next to the flagpole?"

"Ben Sheffield Sr.," Paul said, "my grandfather. He's holding up a pamphlet of his twenty-point plan."

"Obviously a pretty important figure," I said.

Paul frowned. "Pretty self-important."

"Paul is being unfair," Melinda said. "Ben Sr. was responsible for much of the economic success and development in Harding."

"Development," Paul scoffed. "You got that right."

"Truth be told, most people liked the old man," Melinda said. "He brought in a lot of jobs, restored a lot of buildings, improved the university, and made the town a tourist site — at least for Pennsylvania."

"Are you praising him?" Abe asked. "The man was a skunk who left his stink everywhere." He high-fived Aphra. "If Glen could hear you--"

"Glen wouldn't deny those things," she said. "For me it's the way he treated his wives, the lack of women on the council and other town committees. I could go on and on."

"Brava," Abe said. "Spoken like a true follower of Stanton."

"Stanton?" I asked.

"Elizabeth Cady Stanton," Melinda said. "Local early defender of women's rights and abolitionist."

"Either way, Tosh and Philip Harding would've thrown his body in the river when he died," Abe said. "Not make a statue of him."

"Oh, c'mon, look at this square," Melinda said. "Like it or not, it's all because of Ben Sr."

"What do you think?" Paul asked me.

I looked at the flowers and shrubs, the beautiful bandstand in the center, all those uniquely painted benches and restored buildings. "Very quaint. But like a fairy tale."

"In which one could never imagine any evil act occurring?" Abe said.

"Then it wouldn't be like a fairy tale," I said.

Droves of residents continued to stream in from every direction. Stationed throughout the square were tables with large posters set up on poles—"Station A," "Station B," and so on, with people lined up in front of them. Guardsmen sat behind the tables with no pleasantries, no smiles, and no time wasted. It reminded me of a prison, with the inmates each handed a bowl and the abrupt message, "Keep movin'."

Since Paul, Abe and Melinda worked in the same area, they were in the same line.

Despite the enormous crowds, it was oddly silent. I would've thought that the assembly might have provided an opportunity for community and some mingling, but it was all business. No one appeared angry, yet smiles were rare.

Only then did I begin to wonder how they would register me, the visitor. I had no card and wasn't on the lists. I thought I might slip away and hide until the registration was finished.

"No, no," Melinda said. "There's nowhere to hide."

"Just wait in line until registration is finished," Paul said.

Abe nodded. "They'll probably give you a special card."

As I looked at the stern men and women behind the tables, I doubted that Abe was right. If they're tough on the citizens, why would they treat visitors better?

"What about the wrist bands?" I asked.

"Well, yes," Abe said, "There's that problem, I suppose. After swiping the citizen cards, the authorities issue wrist bands – a different colour for every day of the week."

Great, so anyone in authority could detect whether someone had missed registration at a glance. "Here's an idea," I said. "Why not just say I've come down the mountain from hiking in the woods, with no prior awareness of the situation?"

"No one's going to believe that," Melinda said. "You can see the orange from the mountain."

"Then what? I can't be honest. I can't hide."

Melinda thought for a moment. "If we show you how to escape, would you help us?" She leaned in close. "You'd need to take Aphra with you."

"And Peirce," Abe said.

I took a step back, laughing nervously.

"Sounds good to me," Paul said.

I stared at them. "You brought me here to use me," trying to control my anger. "But you don't know me, remember? I wandered in from nowhere. For all you know I could hate children and pets. I could be a murderer!"

Paul smirked.

Was their attitude also part of their sickness? Like the others, I was beginning to blame the orange. I turned and started to walk again toward the park. I had to reach the mountain.

In moments Melinda was beside me.

"Look," she whispered. "No one knows what this orange is, and I don't want my only child to find out. Look at you. Your eyes water, you can't breathe. Perhaps we're all part of some experiment gone wrong. I'm sorry. I'm afraid for my daughter."

"I only stopped for directions. Besides, wouldn't Aphra be missed in the registration?"

A Guard blocked us. "Get back in line please."

Seeing no other option, I followed Melinda back to the line.

"Children aren't registered," she said.

"Neither are dogs," Abe said, holding on to my arm. "Please. He's the healthiest puppy I've ever seen!"

"Why don't you take him away then?"

"We can't leave Harding when it's like this," Melinda said. "But my little girl? The puppy? They don't deserve this."

Another realization broke through the mental haze. This registration system wasn't only to keep track of people in Harding; it was to keep people loyal.

"Can't you see we're desperate?" Paul said. "We want our city back."

My first instinct was to escape. But I also believed that Melinda was right: this was no place for a child. Peirce reminded me of Rusty, the stray I found in the mountains.

"We'll make certain you've enough money to take care of them," Paul said. "Just go to the hut."

"You must hurry," Melinda said urgently, grabbing my arm. She took another route this time, going behind the Guard to reach the west wall of the building where the crowds were far denser. She gestured for me to continue on that way, staying concealed along the wall, while she rushed back to the others.

Such pathetic pleadings. But we both agreed on one thing: Staying in line was unsafe. I had to get away from the square.

Chapter 4

Part of me wanted to stay and find out what would happen but escape now looked more and more attractive. I edged along the building on the west side of the square. Meld in with the crowds, Melinda had said, until you reach the park. Then all I had to do was retrace the path I'd taken with Paul.

Yet first I had to slip out of the square, even though I felt like a dandelion on a putting green. I tried to calm myself and act as if I was familiar to citizens and the Guard. One step at a time. Concentrate on something else. Like where would I get a flashlight for the tunnels?

Melinda and Aphra had returned to Paul and Abe in the line. I stayed in the shadows underneath a balcony, a short distance from the café. From there it was only a few steps on the road that led to the park. People were looking in my direction – it was all I could do not to bolt.

Melinda leaned down to Aphra, handed her a few items, and pointed in my direction. Aphra looked at me and nodded. On the far side of the park, the bridge beckoned. I started toward it without looking back.

Residents were still walking toward the square. They stared at me as I passed, but no one stopped to talk. I rolled my sleeves down to cover my bare wrists.

The park and one of the golden grasshoppers were ahead. I quickened my pace. Halfway to the bridge, I glanced over my shoulder. A small group of guards had just turned from the square into the road.

Had Paul, Abe or Melinda given me away? I began to run. The park was all open space; the shrubs wouldn't hide even a child. Worse, the bridge was guarded by a National Guard soldier. The guard, with a German shepherd on a leash, stopped me with a kind tone.

"Ma'am, what's wrong?" he asked. "You can't go this way." The dog's big black nose sniffed me.

"That's fine."

"Could I see your identification?"

I showed him my driver's licence. "I was lost and accidentally entered the town."

"You need to head back to the square and talk to the officers at the stations."

I turned around and saw another Guard enter the park.

"Stop her!" one of them yelled.

The Guard with the dog grabbed my arm and began to lead me over to them. We hadn't gone more than a few yards when I saw Aphra and her mother entering the park. They hugged and Aphra broke away and raced down the eastern path along the river's edge, heading north. Melinda signaled frantically for me to follow.

I hesitated for a moment, ripped my arm away from the officer, and raced off as fast as I could after Aphra. Fortunately, my action seemed to surprise the Guard and his dog, who didn't immediately pursue me. The other Guard wasn't so fooled. I could feel him close behind. Never had I moved so quickly. I can only imagine how it must have appeared – a girl in a short skirt and blouse running as if a tiger was after her, a woman close behind, and a couple of Guards not far behind the woman.

We ran up the path to a place where the river narrowed. Without a moment's wait, as if she had done it many times, Aphra threw off her shoes, jumped into the river, and began to swim across. The heavy sound of military boots was coming down the path. I had no choice but to leap in.

Warning shots were fired. The dog barked. Aphra was already halfway across the river. I'm not an especially fast swimmer, but with adrenalin flowing I was moving faster than usual. Out the corner of my eye I saw Guards running toward the bridge.

Aphra reached the shore and raced off into a junk yard. By the time I hauled myself out onto the muddy bank, I could no longer see her. The yard was scattered with drums, old cars and trucks, cement sewer pipes, huge plastic barrels and countless other discarded items. I looked back and saw two Guards swimming across the river, while others were running up my side of the riverbank.

"Stop! You're under arrest!"

More warning shots.

Then a little voice below me spoke: "In here."

Aphra was peeking out of a long cement pipe. I crawled into it and followed her down several others until we met a tunnel. She held out her hand and led me with a flashlight through several minutes of near darkness. I saw very little but heard the kissing squeaks of rats and smelled a damp odor like an old basement. That tunnel met others going in different directions, but Aphra seemed to know the way. Soon I saw a distant circle of orange light.

When we crawled out, we were near the backyard of her home. Peirce was tied up next to his doghouse. When he saw Aphra, he began barking.

Dripping wet, we briefly sat on the back stairs of the duplex to catch our breath.

Aphra was smiling widely. "We did it!"

"Yes, we did."

"C'mon. Let's get my stuff and change. Mummy says you can use her clothes."

When I didn't move, she asked, "What's wrong?".

"I'm sorry," I said. "I'm going on alone. I can't take responsibility for you and Peirce."

The happy expression on her face disappeared. "We'll follow you," she said in a defiant voice. "I know how to reach the hut and Paul gave me a key."

My mind froze. Once again, I found myself in a corner. Like that time in university when I was one of the leaders giving the speeches and encouraging others to protest the university's weapon research, until the campus police came, and I ran.

"I'm not going to the hut, Aphra. I'm sorry, but--"

"--I know," Aphra said. "You'd not good with kids and dogs. Mummy said I might have to take care of you."

"Really?"

"It's OK. She trained me. Glen trained me." She gazed longingly back at Harding.

What would a mother have to say to induce a child to leave her for a stranger? If Aphra can face this situation, I thought, why can't I?

Aphra untied Peirce, picked him up and cradled him. "Don't worry, we can do it."

"Don't you worry either," I said softly. "She'll be fine. She has friends."

*

After we had changed into dry clothes, we gathered the items we needed into two backpacks and one small satchel. We made our way through the same tunnel and cave that Paul and I had traveled, a passage that Aphra appeared to know well.

The trip was not without tears. Seemingly oblivious to the dank environment, Aphra would suddenly stop, her flashlight pointing at the ground, and whimper. I hurried her onward through the claustrophobic tunnel crawling with snails, grubs, and worms. I yearned for the light and was relieved when we left the cave.

Because Aphra was so distraught, I suggested we spend our first night at the hut. Yet even that distance was too far. As her eyes filled again with tears, she told me she wanted to sleep on the hillside overlooking Harding. I doubted the Guard would follow us in the dark, so I accepted the risk.

It was a warm and cloudless summer night. I found an area under a large fir tree. Peirce and Aphra cuddled together and I rested on the other side of the trunk, making a pillow of bags.

"Can't we sneak back in?" she said after a time.

"I'm sorry, Aphra. You're safer here."

She started to sob quietly. "I want Mummy."

"Don't worry," I said. "You'll see your mother soon."

When she finally fell asleep, all was quiet except for the slight wind passing through the trees and the periodic snore of a puppy. If we were ordinary campers, it would have been an inspiring moment. We were high above the city and valley below. The lights of the houses were glittering. We could smell the dogwood, pine and many wildflowers, especially the grape odor of the Eastern Shooting Star. The river glistened as it flowed by the city. Towering around us were the mountains. All of it sunk deep into the cushion of an orange cloud.

Chapter 5

I awoke first and watched what was happening below. The people were marching again from all directions into the square. From this distance, the ritual was even more alarming.

"I'm thirsty," Aphra said, sitting up beneath the tree. Peirce stirred.

"Well," I said, "there's no water around here."

"There's a stream nearby." She ran a short distance to a tiny underground stream that flowed out of the mountain.

"I'm sure it's polluted," I called out, recalling the stream near the hut.

"It depends how much you drink."

She made a cup with her hands and slurped the water before I could stop her. Beside her Peirce licked a little too.

"Mr. Jones has been drinking it all his life," she added, "and he's all right. Here." She held some water out to me in her dirty hands.

"No, thank you. I'm going to find water I know is clean."

I began to gather up our bags.

"Glen would know," she blurted.

"Well, he's not here. Do you know where he gets his water?"

"From certain caves and underground springs."

"And where are they?"

She shrugged and turned her face away.

We began the walk up to the hut.

"Are we going to see Mummy today?" Aphra asked after less than five minutes on the trail.

"No."

"What about Peirce?"

I stopped and turned around to face her. "What about him?"

"When is Peirce going to be with Abe?"

"Come over here," I said softly. I set down the bag and squatted. She walked over and stood before me. Arms at her sides, she rocked back and forth as if she was moving to some inner melody.

"Look, I'm the one who had to leave. You could stay, but your mother thinks it's not a good idea. Believe me, you're going to be with her just as soon as possible."

"When?"

"Not until the orange lifts. OK?"

She nodded. I gave her a quick hug. She turned and started walking again.

We continued our trip without any sign of a path. Aphra clearly recognized certain trees, and other landmarks from her journeys with Glen. The climb was arduous. Periodically we would put down the bags for a few moments. Aphra would glance back down into the valley, hoping, I suppose, that the orange would start to dissipate.

When we reached the large rock slab that Paul had sat on, we stopped for a longer rest. Peirce ran loops around us, sniffing and investigating everything. Aphra hopped up on the stone.

"I've been watching the way you walk," Aphra said.

"Now why would you do that?"

"Mummy calls you Poise," she said.

"Really?"

She giggled.

"She calls Paul 'Star,' because he has this tattoo. Abe is 'Pillow' because of his belly; Glen is 'Eagle' because of his narrow face, eyes and nose. You're Poise because of the way you walk."

"It's the ballet lessons," I confessed. "I spent years walking around on toes with my back curved back, my knees turned out. It makes you aware of your body. When my feet were normal they were also facing outward. What about Tosh, any nickname for him?"

"Nope."

"And Peirce? Where'd he get his name?"

The puppy had picked up a rotten piece of wood. He was carrying it around as if he'd caught his prey.

"He was named after some philosopher."

"I like the name Aphra. Did your mother make it up?"

"It's a good thing Mummy's not here. Aphra Behn is really important to her. She was a writer and playwright who lived in the seventeenth century. And guess what?"

I shook my head.

Aphra leaned close and whispered, "She was a spy!"

"Wow. Quite remarkable for a woman back then."

"Girls can do anything," she said, swinging her legs beneath her. "And you know what else? Mummy found a man just to have me. She didn't want a husband, she wanted a child."

I smiled and nodded. Her mother was quite a woman too, I thought. I wondered who she had selected as the father.

"'Men aren't bad,' Mummy says. 'They're primitive.'"

"I guess it's a good thing I'm not a man."

"She wouldn't have let me go if you were. She didn't even want me to leave with Paul or Abe."

"What about Glen?"

"I wish! I love it when Glen babysits. We have so much fun. But Mummy said he can't leave."

I assumed Glen's feelings were similar to those of Paul and the rest: stay to support the town. I was hoping nonetheless to meet him. My father was always at home in the woods too.

"What are we going to do now, Poise?" Aphra said after a moment.

I stood up. "Food, water and shelter."

*

The hut was a one-room wooden structure, unfinished but livable, with kitchenware, four cots, and a rug by the woodstove that Peirce immediately assumed was his. Caulking and insulation around the two windows were barely adequate. Light shone through a couple of small holes in the roof and slats in the floor. I blocked the gaps with pieces of firewood and stuffed some socks around the windows. Not as rough as camping, but not somewhere I would want to spend a winter. Despite the minimal comfort, I was relieved not to have the orange cloud hovering.

Aphra sat on a cot and held up a wrinkled piece of paper with barely legible scribbles on it. It was a list of chores.

"This is silly, Aphra. It's only one room. And we may not even stay."

She took the note back and began ironing out the creases on a cutting board. I sat down beside her and Peirce jumped up to lie on the other side.

"It doesn't matter. Even if we're here for a week. Who will do the dishes? And the sweeping? And clean clothes and linen?"

"Okay, we'll take turns."

"Fine."

She checked those items off the list and put the bread board on the floor. Peirce laid his head on her lap. She petted the top of his head and scratched his ears.

"What about looking after Peirce?"

"The puppy's your responsibility."

"Not fair."

"I never wanted him to come along."

She gently grabbed Peirce's face in her hands.

"She didn't mean that, Peirce. Look at that face. How could you not want him here?"

"OK," I said, "I'll take him out at night if he has to go. Otherwise, he's all yours."

"I'm glad Peirce can't understand you."

She stood up and went to the tiny kitchen area, opening the few cupboard doors.

"Now, the fun part, shopping for food and cooking!"

"You can cook?" I asked.

"Of course. Mummy has shown me how to take care of myself. There's a store up the road. Glen and I have been there. And Mummy gave me money"—she revealed a wad of bills from her backpack. Next, she dug out a grocery list. We walked to my car, leaving Peirce behind in the hut.

The store had once been part of a gas station. The old pumps, the air dispenser, and the side garage were still there, as well as the outside entrance to the washroom. I could still smell the grease and the rubber from the tires displayed out front.

There were no other customers. A middle-aged woman dressed in Bermuda shorts and a loose-fitting colorful blouse stood still as a mannikin behind the counter. My first thought was that she had just returned from a trip to Florida. As we walked by her, I smelled a heavy dose of perfume. She nodded, gave a little wave to Aphra, but said nothing.

After we shopped for a couple of minutes, she appeared directly behind us, making me jump.

"Can I help you with anything?" she said in a low voice.

"I think we'll be fine."

"Where's Glen?" she asked Aphra.

Aphra shrugged.

"He was in here the day before yesterday. Strange fellow. Comes in, looks around, and buys nothing. I asked him why and he said, 'Just wanted to make sure you're OK.' His father knew my grandfather. They would go off to these native rituals together. My grandfather was part Erie, you know."

She followed us as we stocked up on necessities and bottled water.

"I miss Grandpa," she said finally. "I've thought of selling, but the folks tell me they need the store."

"Sure I can't help you find anything else?" she asked as she cashed us out.

I shook my head.

"Well, you come back soon. Say hello to Glen, Aphra."

On the way out to the car, I looked and saw her standing frozen at her place.

As I was driving back, I had a fleeting impulse to take Aphra and Peirce someplace far from Harding. But the orange now felt more like a test than an adventure, an even stronger motivation to stay.

Back at the hut, we unloaded the car. As Aphra made her way to the door, I glimpsed someone disappearing down the mountain path.

"You go in," I said, "I need to grab some wood."

I surveyed the area cautiously, not wandering far from the hut. No one was visible, but a pair of deep footprints showed the person had stood for a while where the path leads down the mountain.

When I walked back into the hut with wood in my arms, Aphra said, "I like it here."

Peirce barked. I half-heartedly agreed, looking past her out the window for any movement in the brush. Smiling down at my charges, I locked the door, sliding the long wooden board into its clamps.

I asked Aphra to sit on the cot with me. "I want to talk to you about something."

"Did I do something wrong?"

"No, not at all. But it's important."

Once again Peirce jumped up beside her. We were like a little family.

"I don't want you wandering around out there without me."

She nodded.

"Promise me?"

"I promise."

"I know you're used to wandering around the mountains with Glen, but we're alone up here and the orange is still out there. We must be careful."

"Don't worry, Poise."

But I was starting to worry how was I going to take care of two little ones. I recalled when Dad and I would camp in the Pennsylvania wilderness and I would look at him the way they were looking at me now. I recalled that unswerving trust.

Chapter 6

Aphra and I both liked to keep busy. To accommodate our imaginations and interests, we developed a chart to catalogue wildlife in the area. Most of the time we searched in the daylight, but there were a few nocturnal discoveries, usually involving the garbage bin. Most often it was racoons, squirrels, rats, though once there was a spotted skunk. One night, after we had closed the windows, I woke to the familiar sound of something trying to conquer the bin. Rolling over, I saw Aphra already at the window, her hand on the latch. She gestured for me to join her. In the moonlight we saw a long-tailed weasel with a thin sleek body, a brown coat above and white belly below, supported by short legs. We noticed it just as it was dragging away a vole.

Each day was the same routine. We would get up before dawn, and spend most of the morning wandering the mountainside, searching, reporting and drawing pictures of what we had seen. I also wanted to see if any changes had occurred in Harding. At about midday, we would bring out our lunch, stare down at the city from different places on the mountain, and talk.

One day we had just finished reporting on a black-capped chickadee. We were at quite a distance from the hut, which rested in the mountains to the northwest of Harding. Our plan was to explore the lower areas first, then expand outward in concentric circles. We had just gone up to a sunlit area.

We sat down on two stumps and were beginning to eat when we noticed a man hiding behind a large protruding rock below. The sight of another human being startled us. Other than the person I had glimpsed when we returned from the store, we were used to being alone.

Aphra hid behind a large fir. "I'm scared."

"Why?"

"It could be the Guard."

"I doubt that. They have enough to do in Harding. Let's see who it is. We'll be quiet."

She shook her head.

"Do you want me to go alone?"

She nodded. "But..."

"But you want me to stay too."

She nodded again.

"OK, tell you what. See that rotten stump up there? We need to add more insects to our reports. You go up there with Peirce, but quietly, and report what you see. They'll be plenty there. OK?"

She agreed and started her climb. I watched her for a minute. Then I descended, moving from tree to tree and staying as low to the ground as possible. Because there hadn't been rain for some time, the grass and weeds were dry. Every step made a noise.

I hadn't gone very far before I heard a sound behind me. It didn't sound like a small animal or the wind. I stopped. It stopped too. I took four steps. It also took four steps. I grabbed a stick and quickly swiveled round.

Aphra jumped from a fir tree and faced me with a mischievous smile. The sight of her brought both relief and delight.

"Scare ya?" she said and walked down toward me. I gave her a pat on her head.

"I don't want to be up there alone," she whispered, holding on to my arm.

We slowly progressed to the shield of a large oak. There was a man bent over doing something with his hands in the soil.

Aphra laughed.

"It's Glen."

I put my finger up to my lips.

"I can't believe it," she whispered. "I'm so happy."

I had to smile when I saw his face. A few days earlier Aphra and I had been walking along a small plateau when we noticed a large bird perched on one of the electrical poles that ran across the hills.

"Wow," Aphra said. "Is it a vulture?"

"No," I said. "I've seen those when I traveled out west with my family." We carefully moved closer. I had never been so near to a bald eagle.

Aphra giggled. I shook my head, but the eagle heard her and flew away.

"What was so funny?" I asked.

"It reminds me of someone."

"Who?"

"Glen."

Now that I could see him with my own eyes, I had to agree. Glen's large, deep-set eyes and long, pointed nose seemed to comprise his entire face. His cheeks and forehead were flat, his eyebrows were thick and met in the center, and his hair was cut close. He had the nervous jerking motion of a bird too, looking about constantly. It also resembled the person I saw near the hut.

"Do you want to talk to him?" I whispered.

"He must know we're here," she said. "These mountains are his domain."

"I suppose," I said.

"I do miss him."

"So...should I...?

She shook her head. "If he wanted to talk to me, he would."

"But he'll tell your Mom we're OK, right?"

She nodded.

The thick shrubs and trees hid him in part. For a moment he went down on his knees as he concentrated on whatever he was doing, then he rose and, with a last look around, rushed away through the trees. We immediately went down to the area. Except for his footprints, the area seemed to be undisturbed.

Naturally I was curious about what Glen was doing on the mountain. I couldn't believe he was only keeping an eye on Aphra for her mother. There was no pattern to when we would see him, but over time it became clear that the locations seemed to be approximately the same distance from the city and from each other. Only on one occasion did we find any trace of him. Under some mushrooms near the entrance to the tunnel we'd used to escape, Aphra found what appeared to be a broken microchip.

I wanted to know more, but my only resource was Aphra. One day we talked while sitting on the edge of the Allegheny, our feet hanging off the bank.

"I don't see any fish," I said.

"You will. Glen calls it a nest."

"Never heard that term."

"Like home for humans. They come back here. Look, there's a Rainbow trout, a small one."

"Check it off," I said. "So, what did you and Glen do together?"

"Nothing special. Play games. Wander through the tunnels."

"Did he make the tunnels?"

"I don't think so. But they go all over the place. Glen showed me how to escape from the downtown to my house, just in case. He has little places in them where he feeds and leaves food for animals. Sometimes he meets people in them."

She lay on her stomach so she could get a better look. "What's that?" Her face was only a few inches from the water.

"Musky, I think," I said, leaning closer to the water.

"Really? They're so long."

"They are. So what did he talk about with these people?"

"I don't know. He spoke in a native language. He was trying to teach me, but I only know a little."

"Did your Mom go along too?"

"Mummy finds the tunnels scary."

"What about Mr. Jones?"

"Sometimes. Look! A Walleye. They're so beautiful." She made a click as if she had a camera.

"Check it off." I caught a glimpse of fleshy whiskers among the weeds and pointed.

She grinned. "Catfish."

"I suppose Mr. Jones knew Glen's father and grandfather too."

"I guess. He's pretty old."

"So what did Glen talk about with you?"

"Stuff. Nature. We would see animals or plants when we were wandering about, but we wouldn't keep track or write about them. He loves the outdoors."

We moved a little farther north to another favorite place of Glen's. Two streams met the Allegheny, creating a V. We sat on a large patch in the middle where the water was almost as loud as a waterfall.

I pulled out our notebook. "What's he like?"

"He's really nice. Kind. Weird sometimes."

"Weird?"

She laughed. "He talks to animals."

"Really?"

"We were in the forest and he saw a fawn. We hid between some large fallen trees. We were very close to the deer. He said to it in a squeaky voice, 'Now Angie, where's your mother? You know it's dangerous alone here.' The deer seemed to hear him and raced off. One time when we came out of one of the tunnels and there was a bear, right in front of us. 'Walto,' he said, 'what are you doing here?' The bear looked at him for a moment, then strolled away." She paused for a moment. "What's that smell?"

I caught a whiff of something weedy and rank. "Algae? Who knows what's dumped in here."

"It happens on the days the factories dump." She put her hand in the water and brought some of it closer to her nose. "I'll tell Glen when we get back."

"Anyway, in the tunnels," she continued, "he'd go into these places where he'd light candles and meditate. He tried to show me how, but it was hard."

"He'd say, 'Sit still and focus on that little light in the far distance of your mind.' I couldn't see any little light, but I didn't want him to be disappointed in me."

"I'm sure he wasn't. Meditation takes practice."

She managed a half-smile. "Hey, where are all the fish? Let's go back to the other place."

"Be patient." I took a breath. "How did he know about the tunnels?"

"I think the native people showed him. There! Isn't that a brook trout?"

"Speckled body, red belly, whitish fins . . ."

"Yep. They're my favorite." She watched it swim away. "Did you know the tunnels even go under the city. He took me everywhere."

"He trusted you."

She nodded, took off her shoes and socks, rolled up her pants, and began to wade toward the middle of the stream. I followed her.

She looked round at me. "One time we were on the other side of Harding, where you can hunt, and he stole guns from the hunters."

"I was waiting at the tunnel entrance. He brought them into the tunnels, and took them to another location, and buried them."

Aphra scooped up a minnow, looked at it, and returned it to the water. "One time he saw a farmer mistreating a horse. Glen took the horse."

"Into the tunnel?"

She looked at me. "No, of course not. To an animal rescue farm for old and abused animals." She smiled to herself. "I adopted a rooster."

"There's a largemouth bass."

"We have it."

I checked down the list. "You're right."

"You know, one time I went with him when he destroyed several machines that sprayed pesticides. He poured acid all over the engine parts."

"He could have been arrested."

"They were hurting the plants!" Aphra said sharply as she walked back to the bank. "And people too—"

"OK, OK, settle down."

"Don't criticize him. Other than Mummy, he's my best friend."

"Sorry. I was worried about you. He's an admirable person, but I just don't want you to get into trouble."

We began putting on our socks and shoes.

"I shouldn't have told you that stuff."

"I won't tell anyone. It's our secret."

"You promise?"

"I promise."

"Glen wouldn't hurt anything. He's even a vegan. I'm going to be like him when I grow up. Mummy won't do it. She said she needs the meat."

Aphra saw several slender and dark goldfish with black fins swimming together where the streams meet the Allegheny. "Is that a black carp?"

"Yep. Check it off. Where does he live?"

"He always comes to our house." She turned around and looked at me with narrowed eyes. "Why do you want to know so much about Glen?"

"Just curious."

"Can we go?" she asked abruptly. "I'm hungry."

*

A couple of weeks passed without us discovering the reason behind Glen's activities. Meantime, the orange hung over Harding as bright as ever. Every morning, the Hardies went to the square past the soldiers posted on the bridge. The risk of re-entering Harding was too high, but the itch to know what was happening was becoming unbearable.

One day, we were exploring on a small hill to the south of the city. We would only go there in the middle of the day when most Hardies were at work. It was high and close enough that Aphra and I could easily peek through the trees with binoculars and see what was happening in Harding.

On that day we saw a large group of people gathered in the city square around a person upon a platform beside the flagpole. The crowd mushroomed until it filled the entire square.

The sight made me nervous. I felt certain the person was going to jump, but I didn't want to say out loud what I was thinking with Aphra there. I grabbed Aphra's hand and we began the long climb up the winding mountain path. Why was this crowd gathering? Who was the person on the platform? We didn't have to wait long for an answer.

Chapter 7

On the Monday of the next week, Harding's oldest citizen, Tosh Jones, visited us. The mass of wrinkles on his dry face, as well as the orange tinge to his skin, was shocking at first. If not for his steady walk and the fire of life in his eyes, I would have thought he was near death.

Aphra took Tosh by the hand into the hut. He sat down out of breath at the table. After a minute or two, he began shaking his head and making sounds of relief, as if a great pressure had been taken off him.

"I need to tell you…" he said, gasping.

"It's fine, Grandpa Tosh," Aphra said. "Lie down and rest."

"But they may be following…Go. Now. Look."

"I will," I said, patting him on his shoulder.

I went to the door and looked out, then returned to him. "No one."

We took him over to a cot, removed his shoes and covered him with a blanket. In a few minutes he was sleeping as if he hadn't slept for a long time.

He was still asleep after Aphra and I returned from our morning explorations. When Tosh did awake, he stood up in a state of alarm, and said, "Quickly! We must go!"

I urged him to sit back down on the bed and explain.

"First we must leave. Then I'll talk."

His destination was a mountain much higher than the ones we were accustomed to. Almost immediately, as we began our climb, Tosh calmed. It was a gentle slope, but it still required stamina. Clearly here was a man who had spent his life roaming in the mountains.

"Before you ask, Aphra, your mother is fine. In fact, that's part of the reason I'm here. She wanted to let you know. And Glen said it was time for me to come to bring you the news."

"Are we going back?" Aphra said, her voice full of hope.

"No, no, I'm sorry, Aphra."

Aphra slumped, disappointed, and stopped to pet Peirce.

"What was that big gathering in the square?" I asked.

"Yes," said Aphra, "what happened?"

"It all goes back to one morning several weeks ago, when we all awoke to notices pinned around the city. It said, 'If you are interested in stopping the orange, come to the square at noon on Wednesday.'

"That sure got us excited. Though to be honest, some thought it was a hoax."

"But it must have brought hope," I said.

"It did," Tosh said. "I was almost giddy."

Aphra pointed at a tree a hundred feet ahead of us.

"I can't believe it," I said. "A Dark-eyed Junco. They're never here in the summer. Check it off, Aphra."

"Shh," Aphra said. "I want to get up close. Here, Tosh, hold on to Peirce. I don't want him to spook it."

Tosh took the leash. Peirce tugged and whined.

I squatted beside him. "Now boy, you know how the birds feel about you."

We circled around the tree so we ourselves wouldn't spook it. We were now directly below the bird so that its white belly was visible.

It jumped up to another branch. and began to sing – a fast whistle with little change in pitch. Aphra tried to imitate it without success.

We high-fived and stood up. The Junco flew off.

"Sorry to stop you, Tosh, but that one wasn't even on our list."

"I understand. Haven't seen one of those myself."

"So what happened on Wednesday?" Aphra asked.

"The government announced a curfew for that lunch period. They claimed some fanatic was planning on bombing the square."

"Did the person appear?" I took my turn holding on to Peirce's leash.

"Glen works at the café in the square. He said no one appeared; there was no bomb. The next week the same notices were pinned in different locations, again the government called a curfew, again used the bomb threat, and again nothing happened. By then we had our doubts."

Tosh stopped to rest on the slope. He massaged his legs and stretched them out. Aphra and I weren't tired, but we sat down beside him. I knew that the next incline would be more strenuous. Peirce was happy to watch a bunch of ants near an ant hill.

"We were so tired of having no answers. Tired of the orange."

"I would've thought a few of the citizens would've showed up," I said.

"After the second curfew, some did protest. But they were too few in numbers."

With a little support from me, Tosh stood up and started walking again.

"Some of them were jailed. Not your mother, Aphra. Probably because she was a friend of Paul's."

"What happened the next week?" Aphra said anxiously.

"Well, Wednesday morning came. Morning registration, everything routine.

"No notices. No curfew. At first we didn't know what to do, but after much discussion the group decided we would return to the square at noon."

"Mummy?" Aphra asked.

"Yes, and Paul and Abe. Many more came in the end. Even the Mayor came out onto his balcony, protected by Guards. The square was alive again."

Tosh stumbled and fell. I helped him to his feet and led him to a log under the shade of several large eastern Hemlocks that stood over a hundred feet. He slowly bent and sat upon it, breathing a great sigh.

"I'll be fine in a few minutes."

We rested for a while, watching Aphra throw a stick for Peirce. Sometimes he couldn't find it so she would find it herself, and Peirce would chase after her, not after the stick. Or Aphra threw the stick in the air and Peirce would jump and catch it in his mouth. They enjoyed this game until a squirrel distracted him. Then Aphra lay on the ground to spy on the lives of small creatures. Her hair melded in with the grass as she stared at white flies, aphids and pine beetles in a chunk of rotted wood.

When we continued, I waited for him to pick up his narrative. Aphra had no such tact.

"What happened next?"

"Well, at exactly noon, we heard this booming electronic voice from the top of one of the buildings: *Silence! Silence! Silence!*

"The crowd became silent. The soldiers were looking in every direction. The voice continued:

> *Why haven't you come? Have you become sheep? For months the government has told you that the orange will disappear! Has it disappeared? No! So now you must prove your courage! You mustn't listen to the authorities! You must listen only to yourselves. I will be here next Wednesday. In person. I will tell you what must be done to be rid of the orange forever.*

"We could see the Special Forces scurrying about on top of the buildings. Many of us also were looking for the location of the voice. Who would broadcast such a message? Someone claimed to have a way to end the orange. Except for me, the others scattered around the square to see if they detected any speaker. I started to walk back and forth in an almost lightheaded nervousness. Some were jumping up and down. Some were yelling, as if the orange had already disappeared. If the Guard and the local police weren't surrounding us, we might have burst into exuberant clapping. Yes, the voice threatened us. Yes, the voice called us cowards. But I didn't care. The sincerity in the voice made me believe there was a chance. I watched the authorities frantically try to find the hiding source for the sound. My neck strained upward watching their search; but then suddenly Glen with Melinda appeared and stood beside me. I said, 'I hope they don't find it.' Glen looked at me and smiled."

Chapter 8

The mention of Melinda and Glen together made me curious.

"How did Melinda and Glen come to know each other?" I asked.

Tosh looked at me. "Let me give you a little background. OK, Aphra?"

Aphra nodded. She wouldn't complain whenever anyone talked about her mother.

"Glen knew Melinda in high school, but a year after Glen began working at the café, he started seeing Melinda more often.

"She'd come at closing time and I'd see them sitting at a corner table. At the time she was helping with the journal and working as an executive assistant. Glen was working on his Harding Chronicles and he would discuss it with Melinda. Melinda was into feminism and the role of women in history."

This section of the mountain was quite steep. Fortunately, it was not a long stretch. Tosh leaned on me to reach the next plateau. When we did, he wanted to stop again for a few minutes.

Aphra brought out a ball and threw it while Tosh spoke. Peirce chased after it and brought it back.

"Rarely did Glen talk about his interests or Harding, at least when I was around."

"Were they dating?" I asked.

Aphra held on to the ball. Peirce kept jumping up and trying to take it from her hand.

"There was no sign of affection, except for hugs when they met and left. So I don't know. A close friendship for sure. Aphra, have you ever seen Glen and your mom kiss?"

Aphra shook her head.

"Then Melinda became pregnant. Occasionally I would see Glen and her walking along the river talking and laughing. After Aphra was born, Melinda found a new job and only rarely came to the café. Since then I haven't seen them together very often."

I glanced at Aphra. Tosh didn't know Glen spent a lot of time at Melinda's home.

"Do you know what Melinda thought of Glen's underground schemes?" I asked.

"She was worried he would be caught."

He sat down on a rock. Around us stood several Red Mulberry trees that were attracting a slew of Tanagers, Warblers and Orioles, the group making a loud but pleasant combination of songs. Tosh was staring at a chipmunk who was staring back. It was sitting on its hind feet chewing on a mulberry. Aphra played catch with Peirce.

"So," Tosh said to Aphra. "Have you seen the four most dangerous creatures of this area?"

"You mean other than man?"

"This girl has been around Glen too long," Tosh said.

"We've seen them all," Aphra said. "Snakes, especially the copperhead and timber; spiders, especially the wolf and the southern black; black bears; and black rats, because of the diseases they carry."

"I tell you, this girl is Glen's little prodigy."

"How long have you known Glen?" I asked Tosh.

We sat on the ground next to him. Aphra stopped her ball play and listened intently.

"Since he was born," Tosh said with some pride. "No Harding like that boy. Thinker. Inventor. Probably more native than not. He loves complex mechanical problems and was always concocting intricate schemes.

"Such as?" I said, handing Aphra the water bottle from my pack.

"Well, he might anonymously supply the evidence a lawyer needs to save some poor fellow who's being cheated. He'll do whatever it takes: hypnosis, magic, even threats."

"Magic?"

"Well, as good as. And he accomplishes these things without any publicity. As far as the authorities know he's just the dishwasher at the City Cafe. I only know about his activities because he shares them with me."

"I've been part of his adventures," Aphra said.

"Yes, of course." Tosh stood up and began climbing again. We followed him for a time to a small plateau that formed a sandy ridge around the mountain. The clouds seemed to be coming closer and the sky was a richer shade of blue. He rested on a rock.

"At first I didn't believe Glen when he outlined these schemes. But when I saw the results, I changed my mind. More than that: I began to worry. He was putting himself at risk. I often feared what he would do next. Since no one was ever physically hurt, I kept silent, but there were many occasions when I couldn't sleep. The intricacy of his schemes was a kind of mania."

"I found them fun," Aphra said, kicking the ridge. "Why is there sand up here?"

"You should ask Glen," Tosh said. "Maybe at one time this was beside a lake."

"I remember when he snuck into the slaughterhouse," Aphra said, handing Peirce's leash to me. "He destroyed all the stun guns and disabled the scalding tanks. Then he broke the latches on their trucks."

"What part did you play?" I asked.

"I helped with the trucks. They had security, but no video, so I went up to the guard and acted like I was lost while Glen was breaking the latches. Look!" Aphra pointed to a cave entrance. "Do you think there are bears in there?"

"Stay back beside us," Tosh said to Aphra.

I shortened the leash for Peirce, who had begun to bark when two bear cubs appeared.

"Oh my gosh," Aphra said.

Aphra joined us just as a black bear followed her cubs. By then we had retreated a respectful distance.

We high-fived and took out our checklist. This was our second bear sighting. The first, a week previous, was a frightening experience because it came upon us suddenly from behind.

Aphra wasn't worried. Glen taught her that bears will ignore her if she has no food, no cubs are around, and if she presents no danger.

The bear raised itself on its hind legs and stared at us.

"Back away slowly," Aphra said. "Give it space."

The cubs gathered around their mother and followed her as she returned to the cave.

We headed in the opposite direction, farther up the mountain.

"Glen is especially protective of bears," Aphra said.

"Why's Glen like that?" I asked Tosh.

"Like what?" Tosh said.

"An activist or schemer," I said.

"Not sure," Tosh said. "His father and grandfather were quiet men—though Jacob, his father, believed he had a special mission. Principles are useless, Glen often says, without action."

Aphra nodded. "I remember once we were at Goldman tunnel-"

"Glen names the tunnels?" I interrupted.

"No, I do. Goldman after Emma Goldman. And there's Wollstonecraft Tunnel, Curie Tunnel, Alexievich Tunnel. A few of Mummy's favorite people."

"Where's Goldman's tunnel?" I asked.

"On the other side of the city," Aphra said. "Near Saddle Ridge Chemical, the pesticide maker. Several times he warned them to stop dumping in the river. But they wouldn't listen.

"He filled several giant jugs with water from the river and labeled it: 'Please drink. Enjoy. It's from the stream next to the factory.' I wrote that. That was my job. He placed them at the entrance to the factory so anyone driving by would see them. Then he anonymously called the media and the company executives. He told the executives if they didn't stop polluting the stream, their kids would be drinking the river water at school." She smiled. "I love that word, 'anonymous.'"

"Did they stop?" I asked.

"Nope," Aphra said. "They put up a huge fence around the property and hired security at the school to watch the water supply.

"But Glen says, 'Never let the earth suffer from human stupidity.' He gave the information—and he had a lot of it—to a lawyer, and the lawyer took Saddle Ridge to court. They settled and stopped dumping."

The sun was beginning to set as we reached the summit. Exhausted, we sat down next to each other—Peirce with his head on Tosh's lap—in a secluded spot surrounded by blue spruce trees where Tosh had spent many hours as a boy. Far below, we could see a hint of our hut, the entire city and beyond. Aphra and I were both on the lookout for animals we hadn't found for our checklist, especially the red fox.

"So, what happened the next Wednesday?" Aphra asked. "Was the speaker there?"

"After the message, the government instituted various emergency laws that prevented us from meeting in any sizable group. Extreme measures due to the so-called madness of the speaker. For your own safety, the edict said, you're required by law to stay away from the square.

"At first most of the Hardies saw these laws as protective measures that had little effect on their daily routine, but the laws did seed a sense of distrust. The longer the people went without hearing the message, the more their feelings changed. Paul and Melinda said they were becoming more afraid. In fact, they admitted that they were quite happy that the government had taken action. No one sane, they said, gets up on a roof top and claims to have a solution for what the best scientists in the world couldn't solve."

"Anyway, Wednesday finally came and the square was empty at noon. There were soldiers stationed around it and on every rooftop. Nothing happened."

"Nothing?" Aphra said.

"Well, the speaker said we needed to show courage. Instead, we had become like children. Despite the general doubt, some of us began to believe perhaps the speaker did have a solution, or at least an explanation. This small hope grew, along with our doubt in the authorities.

"The more we thought about what appeared to be official ignorance, the more we hoped for help elsewhere. The voice from the roof was always in the back of our minds.

"How it started, I don't know. But the word began to spread: Why not appear on Wednesday in the square? So Paul, Melinda and I went to Ben Jr. with a petition signed by many residents requesting that the authorities allow people to gather in the square.

"We met him in one of the rooms off the council chambers. He laughed at us.

'Do you think that I'd give you permission to kill yourselves? Before you believed it was the voice of a madman. The situation hasn't changed. We know you're frustrated. So are we. But trust me, the orange, will fade away.'

"'The government has tried but failed,'" Paul said. "'Allow the people to decide.'

"But Ben Jr. just laughed. 'Don't you think it's possible that we have access to information that you don't? Let us do our jobs.' He stood up and went to the door. 'I have other appointments. This is a crisis. Please take yourselves and the crowd you came with and leave, or I'll call security.'"

"What a jerk!" Aphra said. "Typical Sheffield!"

"Up till then we still assumed that the government wouldn't hide anything from the people.

"Some of us decided to stay in the office reception area. Others left and informed our supporters about the results of our meeting. The square began to fill up with those who agreed with us, as well as with those who were just curious. The police arrived with the Guard at the office. We were warned again and told to leave.

"Those who signed the petition were now ready to take a chance. Many were model citizens who wanted to eat, sleep and work as they had always done, but it wasn't the same. Nothing's the same when people wake up and wonder: Will the orange be there? It was wearing us down.

"The police forcibly escorted us from Ben Jr.'s office out into the square. We might have gone home then and there but we felt as if we had nowhere else to go, as if this was the last alternative. I don't think we were particularly courageous. We froze up against the east wall under the balcony. We had no inkling what would happen next.

"Then Glen slipped away. Perhaps he was worried we might stop him. He found his way high above the people to the platform next to the flagpole."

Chapter 9

Glen stood on the platform and looked down on the crowd below. His thoughts were not of them or what he would say or do. Nor was he worried about the Guard. He could see his friends down there under the balcony, but they were protected and would be fine.

From above, the square seemed so small, yet his whole life involved in some way its space and the buildings surrounding it. Even the statue of Ben Sheffield Senior, so near at this height he could almost touch it, pointed to events in the life of his family.

His eyes were drawn to the courthouse where Philip, his grandfather, had used his life savings to take the State to court for ignoring the Harding Promise. Glen had often listened to his father and grandfather speak of the case. The lawyer had argued that the original pact with the Chief was a legal document that should have given the Hardings the power to stop anyone who could potentially harm the area.

The State counsel had argued that the Hardings must accommodate everyone who wishes to use the land.

"As long as they care for it," the Harding counsel said.

"The meaning of 'care' is open to interpretation," the State counsel countered. "Would putting hundreds or thousands out of work be a caring act?"

Philip Harding sat beside his counsel in a state of controlled frenzy. Inside him burned a terrible anger that seemed to have been brewing for centuries in the Harding soul. The stories he had been told and had in turn told his own son Jacob were no more than stories. The natives lived in a restricted area. The number of toxins in land, water and air was growing. If the old Chief could return from the dead, he would damn Hans Harding and all his descendants throughout eternity.

Philip smashed his hand down on the table. "Can't you see we only want what's right?! We're not interested in money! We don't want power! We want to protect our community, our children."

He lowered his head and said quietly, "You'll all pay for this, I tell you. You doom the whole valley," And then to his lawyer: "We don't need a judge. We need an army!"

As Glen stood there, with the people looking up at him, the wind trying to push him off the platform, and the sun hotter than it felt on the ground below, he could visualize his grandfather and a little boy—his father—coming out of the courthouse together into the rain. For the rest of Jacob's life, the cynical grumbling of Philip and the complaining of Jacob's mother Doris filled the house: two hot irons that refused to cool down. Daily they would rage about the betrayal of the Promise. The river, the school, the design of the downtown, the new homes up in the mountains, the restored barns—eventually there was no improvement or change about which they didn't protest.

Jacob was too young to understand that his parents were trying to console themselves. They saw the court debacle as an end, a betrayal of the trust that the Chief had given to their family. To Philip the moral and natural fabric of Harding society was disintegrating.

Glen teetered on the platform. Remembering that court case always led to other painful memories, such as the night when his father came home drunk from one of his binges and burst through Glen's bedroom door, ranting about the time he was taken to the square for ice cream.

Glen looked down upon the bench and imagined his father sitting beside his parents. He could almost see the boy relishing the cone.

"Now, listen carefully, Jacob," Doris said, and Philip nodded. "We want you forget the Harding Promise, and not only that, we want you to forget your aboriginal heritage. Forget what the Hardings tried to do for so many generations."

Jacob looked at them, confused. "But at school I told everyone-"

"Forget it, son," Philip said. "In fact--"

"Philip, I don't think we should," Doris said.

"The boy should know."

"What is it, Daddy?"

"We're thinking about changing our name," Philip said.

"But we're Hardings."

"We also may leave and live somewhere else," Doris added.

Jacob had told Glen this ice cream story several times, sober and drunk.

"First they create this martyr image," he yelled that night, "then they tell me to discard it. As if I didn't get enough mud splattered on me as a Harding kid in that Sheffield swamp."

In the end his parents tried to reel back their words—they didn't change their name or leave—but that day refused to sink into Jacob's unconscious. He took his parents' surrender to heart.

Glen shook the image of Jacob as a child from his head, only to face the teenage version. It was early morning in the square, when the police found his father high on cocaine sprawled out on the grass beside his girlfriend.

"I'm a Harding!" he boasted. "You can't arrest us! This town is named after me!"

"That's right," the girl said, falling down in front of the officers. "He's a legend!"

"What's your name again?" Jacob asked her.

"Jody."

Glen heard that name in the wind wherever he went.

"Jody," Glen spoke out loud under his breath as he stared at the grass far below. A few days after his birth, his mother left town, telling Jacob that she wasn't ready to settle down. Jacob, in jail for disorderly behavior, didn't seem to mind. His own parents assumed the care of the new Harding.

Yet, as Jacob would later explain to Glen, "His eye is on the sparrow." Two years after Glen's birth, Jacob crossed over to what some might see as the other extreme. After meeting and marrying a pious Christian woman who ran the local Alcoholic Anonymous meeting, Jacob created his own version of the Christian faith. God, he believed, was giving him permission to preach the Harding Promise and assist in cleansing the people of Harding of their bad habits.

Every weekend the square became a sanctuary for this new Jacob. After working all week in various seasonal jobs, he would proclaim the good news of Jesus, customized to include the Harding Promise.

Glen, often unnoticed because he was so small, stood next to his father, holding on to his coat, watching the shoppers and busy residents crowding the sidewalks. Just as Jacob had listened to Philip rant, Glen now listened to Jacob.

"You all reside here, but you don't really live here. If you did, you would care about the air you breathe, and the creatures that live off the land with you.

"Look what we've done. Look at factories spewing out filth! Look at that mountainside stripped of its trees. The land is groaning. Can't you hear it? Frogs and bees and butterflies? I'll tell you. It's no secret. They're disappearing before our eyes.

"What do you do all day long? Do you try to learn, to develop skills, to perform acts of kindness? How much have you, sir, created lately? When is the last time you, ma'am, did a good deed?"

Glen gazed down upon that place where the two sidewalks met and saw himself beside his father. How proud he was to be there. He couldn't wait for each weekend to stand in the heart of the city, to feel the excitement of the crowds and listen to his father's mighty words. By the time he was teenager, though, he saw the experience in a different way.

"You father is seriously nuts," a classmate told him at school. "He said my father would have to answer to God for spraying our corn."

"Yeah," said another boy. "He used to be a drunk and drug dealer. Now he thinks he can tell Mayor Ben what to do. What an idiot! People scream at him, but he just keeps talking."

In Glen's senior year the principal asked him to speak on Founder's Day. Glen talked for one hour about the Harding history, beginning with Hans in the seventeenth century. He spoke with great conviction and confidence about the Chief, the Harding intermarriages with the natives, and the many times when his family had tried to protect the flora and fauna of the area.

While the speech proved he knew his heritage, it didn't change the general opinion about his father.

"Go home, you drunk," was a common refrain.

"What do you know about God or goodness? You've spent more time in jail than you have preaching!"

"Where's the squaw for your kid, huh?"

Glen worried that someone would go beyond words and try to injure his Dad. On a bench near his spot on the square, he tried to convince his father to retire.

"Who would stand here for God?" Jacob said. "Who would tell them that love means caretaking?"

"I will, Dad. I know what to say."

"That's brave of you, Glen. You're a good boy and I'm proud of you. But this is my way, not yours."

"But Dad, you should read the history, show them the facts. Otherwise they'll make us look foolish."

"Better the foolishness of God than the wisdom of men."

"But Dad, you've done it for years. You've made your point."

"Have I? Do you see any change?"

Glen looked down upon the growing number of people below. Even now he could hear his father's voice.

"I know what you're thinking, Glen. You're thinking: I can't do this forever. I want you to go to university and find a better way out of this. Your grandfather went to court, and they didn't hear. I preach my faith. Do the people hear me? You must find your own way."

How wonderfully stubborn his father was, Glen thought. Regardless of the weather, Jacob would be there, on his corner. His hair turned gray, but his words and hopes were the same. He never lost his passion or his faith. He never fought back when the people mocked him.

Then another memory demanded attention: the day Glen's grandmother Doris came to listen to her son preach.

Jacob took her tears to mean his sermon had moved her. She knew Jacob was no preacher; he was not even a charismatic person. Jacob was a quiet boy doomed by his father's bitterness. What she was seeing was the end of the line.

It happened as suddenly as Jacob's conversion. In the middle of one of his homilies, he suffered a rapid series of strokes. Glen saw his father staring listlessly ahead, his lips moving to unknown words. A few listeners were laughing. Glen took his father's hand and led him home.

Jacob eventually stopped speaking altogether. Soon he couldn't swallow. When his mouth closed his heart died. The weight of history had been too heavy a load for his gentle spirit to bear.

A final memory brought tears to Glen's eyes. He recalled going to the square after his father's burial, the rain striking his face as he stood in the place where his father had preached for so many years. He gazed up at the tall statue of Ben Sheffield Sr., the mayor who was most responsible for the way Harding had developed. The statue stood on the spot where the pact between the Hardings and the Chief had occurred. Glen thought then as he did now, Why is there no statue of the Chief?

*

When the people saw Glen on the platform, Tosh told us, they wondered if he was going to jump. I too had the same thought when I first saw him through the binoculars.

Now, sitting beside Tosh, Aphra and Peirce high above the city, the same thought recurred.

"So did he...?" I asked.

Tosh was about to answer when Aphra interrupted.

"No," she said. "He went up there to stop the orange."

Chapter 10

I stared at Aphra. "What do you mean?"

"He told me," she said in a casual manner. "Could we go back now? I'm hungry."

"Glen told you he was going up there to stop the orange?" I asked.

She nodded. "He told me not to say anything until Tosh comes."

"Wait, you knew Tosh was coming?" Tosh and I looked at each other.

"Uh-huh. Glen planned it all. Without him, we would never have escaped."

"Do you know how he got up there?" Tosh asked.

She started to walk. "Come on. I'll explain on the way. I want to get home and eat."

Tosh preferred to take a longer but less strenuous route back along the ridge. It sloped toward a path that led directly down to the hut. It would have been difficult to climb, but it was far less exhausting to hike down, because he could hang on to branches. Unfortunately, it was difficult to observe Harding through the tall, thick firs.

"I was the lookout while Glen installed the mechanism in the pole and wired it up," Aphra said proudly. "There was a bracket attached to the mechanism. It slid up and down along the split he cut up the pole. The platform fit on to the bracket."

"But why go to so much trouble?" I asked. "Why not talk from one of the balconies?"

"He wanted to get everyone's attention," she said, as if it was obvious. "And it worked."

As we walked back, we took Peirce off leash. At first, he ran around us in a circle, as if chasing his tail in a burst of wild energy. After a couple of minutes, he suddenly stopped and crouched low, pointing straight ahead. Sitting in a flowering dogwood ahead was a grey fox. No doubt, it was seeking its red berries. But when a ruffed grouse appeared on the ground nearby, the fox sprang down from the branch. The grouse rushed into the brush with the fox chasing after it, and Peirce not far behind. I could hear Peirce's barks for a while. Then they stopped. A minute later he was bounding back to us, his fun ended.

"You're right, Aphra, it did," I said. "What a sight it must have been!

"It was dramatic, all right. He wore jeans in this long black coat and sunglasses," Tosh continued, "and an orange shirt. The scene seemed almost supernatural, as if he was floating in an orange cloud. Shortly after he reached the top, hundreds of sheets filled the air like propaganda flyers dropped from fighter planes. He waited for people to grab the papers. Then he began to speak.

"At the same time police and soldiers were gathering in a corner of the square and appeared as confused as the citizens. If they had suspected Glen, they would have imprisoned him before that day. They had the power under the emergency laws."

Tosh stopped for a moment, leaning up against one of the fir trees, and unfolded a sheet he had stuffed in his pocket.

"I have one here. 'Weeks ago, you heard a voice calling out to you from the rooftop. It promised that it had the answer if you had courage. But you were afraid. You preferred to listen to others, those who called the man a threat. You believed they could solve the mystery of the orange. But has anything changed? Who can affect the orange? You! Only you.'"

Aphra was walking ahead of us mumbling the same words to herself. When we caught up to her, she quickly stopped, her face turning red.

"You know this speech?" Tosh asked.

"No...I..."

"We heard you," I said.

She turned away, squatting to tighten shoelaces that didn't need tightening.

"He wanted me to remember it."

I exchanged a glance with Tosh. "Tosh saw a Queen snake."

Aphra shook her head. "It might have been an eastern garter snake. I've seen them on the slopes."

"Oh, you're right," Tosh said. "I confuse them."

We resumed our walk through the heavily wooded section. Aphra walked ahead, holding Peirce by his leash. Occasionally she kicked some leaves or threw a rock.

"Has Glen ever seen a massasauga rattlesnake?" I called out to her.

"No. He thinks they're gone from our area."

When we reached an open area, Tosh sat down and asked Aphra if she would like to continue the speech from memory or if he should continue reading.

"No, you go ahead."

"'Listen carefully,'" he read aloud.

"'Each of us must no longer work to keep the old businesses and institutions of this city alive. They haven't helped us to change and grow and create. You know what I mean! You know what has become boring to you, what no longer fulfills you. Money, ego, reputation.

"'You're more than a bunch of institutions, You're in a community with all living things.

"'Let the oil pumps be our reminder. They have drained the resources and caused pollution and corruption. Like them, our institutions too must stop and rust away. Let us maintain only what is essential for the development of our bodies, minds, hearts and spirits. At the same time let us not harm any living thing!'

"Glen stopped speaking for a minute. I think he was preparing for the important sentences to come.

"'Every day that we do these things, the orange will diminish. Go home. Ignore the demands to build Ben Jr.'s airport, his conference center, his next chemical factory. Do what is essential.'"

Tosh paused, looked up at the sky and struggled to his feet.

"We need to move on, or it'll get too dark."

We were also hungry and thirsty.

"If we're lucky, we'll see a white-tail." Aphra said. "Glen and I saw a fawn alone last summer at about this time."

"Or...?" I teased. "Your favorite mammal? What did we see a few weeks ago?"

A big smile came on Aphra's face. "The snowshoe!" she said. "I love their hind feet and ears."

"Rabbits?" Tosh scoffed.

"They're not rabbits," Aphra said. "Snowshoe's a hare."

We had entered the densest section of the woods, close to the path that would take us down to the hut. Alone, I would have become lost, but Aphra knew the way by the different trees that served as markers. We quietly followed Aphra as she looked for snowshoes.

"They tend to stick in the same neighborhood," she whispered. "It was right around here."

We stopped and squatted, hidden behind branches.

"Look," Aphra said. "I don't believe it,"

Deep into the forest a bull elk was feeding on some low-lying foliage.

"Look at the size of those antlers," Tosh said in awe.

"What a beautiful animal," I said.

"Oh well, no snowshoe, but an elk," Aphra said, standing up, the elk darting away. "Let's go. I'm starving."

Tosh grabbed on to Aphra's arm and together they navigated down through the great pines. I followed close behind, taking care to avoid the exposed roots of trees, and dead materials from the trees.

"So, Tosh," I said. "What happened?"

"The Guard were forming a wide semicircle around the crowd," he said, his voice echoing through the forest. "Glen reached into the inner pocket of this coat. Some woman screamed: 'It's a bomb! He's got a bomb!'

"Panic ensued. People tried to escape the square, but there was no space to move without shoving and trampling someone.

"'I have no bomb,' Glen shouted, showing the crowd that the object was in fact only a mirror. They began to calm themselves.

"An officer aimed the megaphone up at him: 'Come down now!'

"When Glen made no sign of moving, someone began shooting. The statue, very close to Glen, was hit. Glen somehow crouched down behind it.

"At first I thought the shooter might be some irate citizen, frustrated by the orange. But soon it was revealed that a policeman was the culprit. His fellow officers dragged him away as he shouted, 'Enemy of the people!'

"The Guards in riot gear created a column and began to shove their way into the crowd toward the pole, pushing people aside.

"They began broadcasting by megaphone:

"'Everyone please clear the square. We will create a corridor. Please leave in an orderly fashion. Clear the square.'

"Normally we would never have ignored the advice of the police, but our minds were in a different state.

"Inspired by Glen's words, some of us began arguing with the police.

"All eyes were on the lonely figure shielding himself by the statue. He hadn't spoken since the shots were fired.

"'Don't be concerned about me,' he called out finally. 'Think of your lives. There is more to come. It will get worse, not better.

"'What happens depends upon whether we change. Don't listen to anyone who obstructs you. Listen to your own inner heart. Retake the world, renew your spirits, turn and march forward to new lives.'

Tosh shook his head. "Many probably thought, Oh no, another crazy Harding. How could we stop working for the institutions we had been supporting all our lives? Regardless what some thought of Ben Jr.'s administration, how could we manage without it?

"'Why are you standing there staring?' Glen cried. 'Leave the square, go home, and do nothing. Contemplate! Meditate! When the time comes, you'll know what to do. You'll know that I speak the truth.'

"Ironically, the officials were saying the same thing: 'Leave the square, leave the square.' Quickly the order was given to change the message. The megaphones now proclaimed, 'Leave the square and return to work. Leave the square and return to work.'

"A group of people, including Paul, Melinda and Abe, found their way to the balcony and began shouting out, 'Go home, do nothing! Go home, do nothing!'

"I made my way to the corner near the café. I wanted to be as close as possible when Glen came down the pole. If he was arrested, I wanted to know where they would take him.

"When groups began to leave the square, soldiers were sent off ahead to set up blockades on the residential streets. With the armed Guard preventing them from heading home, people had no choice but to return to work.

"Glen slowly began to descend on his platform. When he reached the bottom, the Guard and the police were waiting for him. He was searched. They found nothing except for the oval mirror. At the same time, the police had apprehended Paul, Abe and Melinda and their supporters on the balcony. All of them were arrested for defying the emergency laws. I followed the police to discover where they took Glen."

Chapter 11

We arrived at the hut just as darkness fell. The moon was clear in the sky. It had been a long day. We were tired and hungry. I prepared some guacamole with tortilla chips and Aphra made burritos with beans and rice. While we ate, Tosh finished his narrative.

"Over the next two weeks, many courageous souls wouldn't register. They remained at home and were apprehended and jailed. But their attitude proved contagious. Others would soon follow their example; and just as Glen had promised, their actions decreased the intensity of the orange. The more change that occurred, the more people stayed home. Even some government employees began to stay away. I was relieved to see Glen's promise fulfilled and wished I could have participated. But I followed Glen's instructions.

"How did Ben Jr. take all this?" I asked.

"Oh, he would stop Glen if he could," Aphra said, between bites.

"You're right," Tosh said. "When the orange started to decrease, Ben took credit for the change. 'We have imprisoned the madman who had threatened the people,' he announced. 'Now we're able to put in motion the means to end the orange.'"

"What an awful man," Aphra said.

"That was his way of trying to be the town savior. Since the day Glen made his speech, no new commercial developments had occurred. Existing businesses and industries had been targeted and given ultimatums. Ben Sr. and his commercial partners had been losing the game.

"The police released Abe, Melinda and Paul. But they were all back in jail the following day for not appearing at their registration. Many others were to join them."

"Is Mummy OK?" Aphra asked. "They won't hurt her, will they?"

"No, Aphra," Tosh said quickly. "She may not be home, but she's safe. The jails are filling up with a lot of tired and impatient people. Since there were no other jails in the area, the city took over old factories and warehouses, and quickly and inadequately converted them with minimal heat and light and barely adequate food. As Ben Jr. constantly explained, 'These people broke the law. People must work. People must register. If they don't, they must pay the penalties. There must be no exceptions.'

"There were indeed no exceptions. The jails became full of whole families, widowers, widows, teenagers, the elderly, the disabled, a few honored citizens, most of them law-abiding people. There were many stories of mothers separated from their children, husbands and wives placed in different jails. Recent immigrants said the hard times they'd had in their homelands were comparable to the situation in Harding.

"Yet the government believed it couldn't back down.

"'We're keeping our citizens safe,' Ben Jr. boasted, 'even if from themselves.'

"By the time I left to reach you here, I estimate that one third of the city was incarcerated. Harding had fallen apart. Ben's regime was losing whatever credibility remained with the rest of the populace.

"As the orange diminished, Glen's stature grew; he's considered a hero by many."

"Yeah!" Aphra said.

"Over and over I heard people repeating the story of him on the pole, how he'd found the secret that the government and its laboratories could not. We named that day Orange Dawn.

"Many wanted to avoid jail, so they disguised themselves, becoming marauders of the night. They bludgeoned police cars, broke windows and doors of government buildings, splattered the statue of Ben Sheffield with various colored paints, and tore up streets with firebombs. Gangs taunted and attacked the Guard and police. Senior government officials had to be escorted to and from work. The 'Orange Dawn' flag, a bright orange sun surrounded by a black background, was raised in the square. The police removed it, but each time somehow it would reappear. It was assumed that secretly a few members of the Guard, police or both were supporting the protest.

"The city was in turmoil and no one was above suspicion. Ben Jr. asked for more troops. Harding, he said, was in an urban civil war."

"After watching the city fall apart, Glen asked me to come up here. I worried about leaving the city. I feared that someone was following me, that I would be placed in one of the camps or factory prisons, even though I wasn't in as much danger as others. I had registered as a retiree and kept out of sight. In any case, I hadn't the stamina to contribute to any protest or to survive the factory prisons, though in my heart I wanted to rebel.

"I felt guilty leaving when my friends were in jail or were afraid to stay in their homes on workdays. But Glen insisted I go. He wanted me to bring Aphra back."

He fell quiet and took up his fork. While he finished eating, I gathered the dishes and began washing them. Aphra stood next to me drying each dish as I passed them to her.

I kept repeating in my mind the chaotic images Tosh told us. Paul had been right when he warned me and suggested that I turn back.

Tosh moved over to one of the cots and lay down, letting out a tired sound of relief. He spoke as he looked up at the ceiling. "The sad truth is that the government is as frightened as the rest of us."

"No one has been hurt," I said, placing the dishes into the cupboard.

"The hurt is cultural. Events in Harding today were unthinkable a year ago."

"Glen says once fear sets in," Aphra said, "there's no return."

When neither of them offered a reply, she brought out the list of animals we had spotted and sat at the table going through them. Beside each name she tried to make a little drawing.

"Look how many we've checked off," she said, showing me the list. I sat down beside her and looked at it. We had a simple organization into plants, mammals, insects, birds and water creatures. The largest group were the plants, followed by the insects, birds, water creatures and finally the mammals. The list made me feel a little nostalgic. I reached over and hugged her.

"Could it be that they do know what's going on?" I asked. "Suppose they caused the orange, by mistake?"

"No," Tosh said, "I think it's their ignorance that's made them paranoid."

"Assuming you're right, how far will they go? Is there some more extreme plan to come?"

Tosh sat up. "Ben Jr. wants to be greater than his grandfather. Maybe he thinks the orange is giving him that chance."

"Glen calls him the snake in paradise." Aphra said.

"He has a plan to deal with Ben Jr," Aphra said, tidily folding her list. "Even when I was little, I had my Amazon dolls and he had his old stuffed animals, and we would battle the Destroyers. And do you know who the Destroyers were? The Sheffields."

Tosh stood up and walked to the window.

"I know where they're keeping him," Tosh said. "Your mother is in the same building. It's the old jail near the river."

"Well, let's do something!" Aphra said standing up impatiently.

"Hold on, Aphra," I said. "We can't just go down there and ask for them. We might be put in prison too."

"We have to be sneaky, like Glen."

Tosh shook his head. "Glen says we must do nothing until it's time."

"What good is waiting!" Aphra shouted.

"I don't know," Tosh said.

The old fellow seemed in a state of confusion. I gestured to Aphra to leave him be, though in my heart I had to agree. Let's go, I thought. Let's get down there and find out what's going on.

Chapter 12

On the fourth day after our return to the hut, Tosh led us down the path to Harding. Aphra and I followed without hesitation. My heart was beating quickly. Peirce was close behind, his tail wagging.

Everything had been planned, Tosh said. Glen had wanted Aphra to be out of danger in the preceding weeks of turmoil, but now he wanted her to experience the events in Harding and to be with her mother.

What he hadn't anticipated was how long desperate people will cling to their old ways. He'd expected them to rebel much sooner after the long months of living under the orange shroud. They had taken much more punishment than he could have believed.

On Glen's advice, we used a tunnel that ended in the basement of a building a few blocks north of the square—the result of an extension that Glen himself had created. The building was conveniently located across the street from the jail where Glen was held.

Several chairs, stacks of new paper, and a copier were in the room.

"Now what?" I asked, as we sat in what appeared to be a large supply room with two chairs and a couch. There was one dim light in the center. Aphra and I sat on the couch. Tosh took one of the chairs.

"Next we tell the authorities that a bomb had been planted in the jail and would be detonated unless they release Glen."

"Seems like a hopeless request," I said.

"Not really, at least in Glen's mind. Whatever the authorities choose, the plan succeeds. If they release him, he's out of jail. If they don't, but are afraid the bomb will kill others, then they'll vacate the building. If they vacate, that opens up the possibility of escape. If they ignore the threats entirely, he has a backup plan, but I'm not sure what that is."

"But there's more, right?" Aphra said.

"Yes, we rally to create a massive demonstration outside the jail."

"We?" I asked.

"Well, not Aphra and I. Glen says I'm too old and he doesn't want Aphra, a child, walking the streets now and facing possible harassment. Aphra and I will stay in the basement to copy and hand out stacks of the flyers to the distributors. Peirce will be tied up so that he doesn't run off."

"Who are these distributors, other than me?"

As in so many of his plans Glen was precise and had considered every detail long before he was jailed. He had arranged for two groups.

"I'm not sure," Tosh said, "how Glen brought together the people in these groups."

"Abe, Paul and my mom helped him," Aphra said.

"Anyway, one group will go out into the city to draw people to a demonstration at the jail by distributing the leaflets and convincing people. Glen partitioned the downtown area into sections. Each supporter takes a section. The other group is to stay around the jail and manage the demonstration."

"Sounds pretty dangerous," I said.

"The police might question or arrest some of you, Glen says, but the police force and the Guard can't be everywhere and shut down every corner."

In this view, Glen had a less positive view of the police and Guard than they deserved.

I selected a section of seven blocks from the corner of Elm and Second Streets to Elm and Seventh Street, approximately six blocks from the jail, and eight blocks from the City Square. Immediately, once out on the street, I noticed that the orange and the chaos had taken their toll not only on the citizens. A certain lethargy or apathy seemed to have fallen on the police and Guard. Several Guardsmen and police walked by me and said nothing. One soldier did stop me, but he didn't mention the curfew and didn't ask for identification. His concern was weapons. Another seemed interested and took a flyer.

Others were less tolerant. On one of my trips, a group of three blocked my way.

"Give us the flyers!" they shouted.

Glen had prepared a little speech for us to repeat. As I handed out the flyers and walked my territory, I said:

"Look around you. Do you see how the orange is diminishing? It's working. Come to the jail to celebrate and demand the release of prisoners."

"It's diminishing because Ben Jr. has figured it out," one of them said.

I repeated my words to others listening to me.

"Those prisoners belong in jail," the harasser shouted back. "They defied the government."

I tried to walk around them, but two of them grabbed me and pushed me to the ground. The other took the leaflets and threw them into the trash.

This happened several times. Supporters sometimes came to my aid.

But not only the attitudes of the people had changed. On my first visit to Harding, the city had the look of a picturesque mountain town, extremely organized and pristine. Every road was watched. The curfew was in force. There was full participation at registration. Now registration was poorly attended because many were confined in the factory prisons. Now there were obvious gaps in the security. Had I not been distributing the protest literature, no one would have paid any attention to me. Outsiders were hardly important now. No building downtown had escaped some sort of defacement. No street was without scars.

I saw dark figures painting on the once glistening white wooden or brick structures. Graffiti covered windows, monuments, and bridges. You could hear the quick slush of the paint brush and then the footsteps running away down the dark streets whose bricks had been smashed with sledgehammers and axes. I saw streetlight posts bent down and bricks being thrown through shop windows. Constantly you would hear glass in buildings and on cars being broken. There were gashes and smashed-in doors and walls. Many streets had no lights. I saw a quaint old police station boarded up and painted with graffiti, then covered, then painted again. Had the building not have its identity carved into its face, I would have thought it was an abandoned building. A police station in the heart of the city was now ready for demolition.

Meanwhile, the orange, though diminishing, remained.

The intensity of the citizens' fury forced me to ask: Did the orange and the policies of Ben Jr. trigger this fury or was this fury ready, with the right catalyst, to burst forth? Something else seemed to be arising from their souls—something seeded long before the orange.

After Tosh dropped off the bomb note and I had distributed my leaflets about the demonstration, I returned to Tosh and Aphra. We waited in the same building several stories above the basement in another room that Glen had arranged—a small empty room whose windows overlooked the jail environs. It was an excellent vantage point to view all the events around the jail.

The Monroe County Jail was a four-story square brick cube, one of the first buildings in Harding. For its time it was one of the largest jails in northwestern Pennsylvania and was often used by sheriffs from other counties. The upper three stories had tiny barred windows, the exit and entrance were down a central stairway. Because of its age, the jail had been upgraded with fire exits on the sides of the building. Once the prisoners reached the main floor, they went down a corridor past two locked gates to reach the exercise yard behind the building. Thus the building had two exits: through the front and through the rear. In light of Glen's plan, where the demonstration consumed the front, he sent the sentries in the rear, around the wall of the exercise yard.

They watched and waited while the demonstration was occurring.

An hour after the bomb note was delivered, the police and the Guard marched out to form a corridor to the exercise yard behind the jail—the precise area Glen had anticipated. Encased by a high brick wall on three sides, the yard was a grassy patch pounded into mostly dirt from the steps of inmates. One by one each floor of the building came out to exercise. The yard was full of Guards and prisoners, including Glen, Paul, Melinda and Abe, the Guards making a thick lining around the walls . Another squad in special uniforms entered the building, with dogs and equipment. Their heads were encased in protective helmets. I assumed their task was to find and dismantle the bomb.

The western wall of the yard was close to the river, across from the beginning of the path Tosh had taken to reach the hut. It was also near, I would learn, the entrance to several tunnels. Glen had concealed the plastic explosives under the ground of the outside wall. It would detonate remotely. When the wall fell to dust, Glen would be gone. A similar plan was being used on the factory prisons. Those walls too would crumble.

"When will it happen?" I asked Tosh.

"I don't know. That's all I know. It's up to Glen."

We could also see a lot of the activity in the front of the police building. The demonstrators had created several long lines of people that wrapped around the building, one behind the other, each holding a sign that said, "Release the innocent," but the crowds chanted, "Justice! Justice! Justice!" In front of them, outnumbered, were two lines of Guard and police, holding up their shields. Behind all of the demonstrators were two flag bearers who had hoisted up large flags bearing the Orange Dawn insignia.

Glen didn't react immediately. He gave the government the opportunity to release him and the others. The authorities didn't relent. His demands were those of a terrorist, Ben Jr. said, and they wouldn't listen to a terrorist.

No one knew who would send the remote signal. The device wasn't with him in the jail. He told no one this part of his plan in case the person was discovered or betrayed him. Later Aphra explained that the person who activated the bomb didn't know she was being used for that purpose. She carried the device unknowingly in her purse, but only Glen could trigger it. He set it off by pressing an implanted chip on his arm.

The sound of the explosion permeated not only the city, but the entire vicinity, setting off a slight tremor and crumbling the western wall. Except for Glen, Abe, Melinda and Paul, all the prisoners were unprepared and the soldiers managed to surround and contain them without injury. Glen and his friends escaped. They vanished so quickly that for a few minutes I thought they was still there in the yard.

Peirce barked. He noticed what we had missed. In all the commotion, Aphra had left our side.

"She's gone into the tunnels after Glen," Tosh said. "Quick! Go!"

I rushed down the stairs and pushed my way through a crowd of people that now surrounded the jail, past some demonstrators and curious bystanders. I saw the tunnels near the river and charged toward them. I assumed that they were the same tunnels Tosh told me Glen and the others had taken.

I was frantic. Why would she leave without telling me? Suppose someone had grabbed her, knowing she was connected to Glen? My heart sank from guilt. Most of all, I imagined her hurt or lost in those tunnels.

When I reached the tunnels, I saw nothing but black space. No left, right or center. Just darkness. If I continued, I would never find my way back.

"Aphra!" I called out. "Aphra!"

There was no answer. I was helpless. I couldn't go forward and I didn't want to give up.

I turned around and saw the mass of people going in all directions. Chaos! A girl wouldn't have a chance in that mob. Darkness or the mob. My eyes began to water. What could I do?

"Aphra!" I shouted once more and slumped to the ground.

I returned to the upper room in a sullen mood.

"Well," Tosh said. "Any sign of her?"

I shook my head.

"She knows the city and the tunnels," Tosh said.

"It's a madhouse out there," I said. "We forget, she's just a child. I should have kept my eye on her."

"Don't blame yourself too much. I'm sure Glen told her what to do."

"How do you know?"

"Because I know Glen, and I know how much he loves that child."

I slumped into a chair. He came over and patted my shoulder. Peirce nuzzled my leg. After a moment I reached down and I petted his head.

Meanwhile those who were escaping from the factory prisons were flooding out into the streets of Harding, across Harding Bridge and up to the mountains. No one seemed to be restraining them, though it would be futile attempt. The police, the prison officials, and the Guard couldn't have penetrated that thick wall of people without injuring hundreds.

Others joined the crowd—folks who had stood by amazed at the events but too afraid to protest, as well as local police. They trusted something would happen when they arrived.

I wanted to stay in the lookout room and hope Aphra would return.

"No, we must leave," Tosh insisted. "We must follow the crowd up the mountain."

"But suppose she comes back and we're not here?"

"Aphra would never come back to Harding in this bedlam. Glen has planned everything in detail. Do you think he'd forget Aphra?"

As soon as the people began to stream out of the city and up toward the mountains, the orange faded rapidly. This realization brought even more people racing up into the mountains. The parade continued for hours. Tosh and I, with Peirce on a leash beside me, marched beside those in prison and street clothes, the Guard, the police, old folk, students, professionals, climbing for their lives. As we reached the top and sat upon the hill side, I saw even Ben Jr. and his family climb.

The streets, buildings, and homes were empty. The gates of all the prisons were open. Soon the air was totally cleared of the orange mist. No one, including myself, could believe it. Silence. Clarity.

Then spontaneously, an immense sound of joy burst from the crowd. They began to hug each other, to clap and dance, making sounds of happiness and relief. Whatever would come next, this moment, this vision of deliverance, I could never forget. The orange was no more. No day was ever so pure.

In the end, thousands of us stood on mountain ridges, looking down upon the city. We could see the square, the shops, the bridges, the schools, the businesses, the factories, and the train station. People could pick out their own homes. Down there stood their old lives, their memories, what they had built, and what they had become. A woman beside me said she couldn't imagine walking the streets again.

So many law-abiding, ordinary people had wanted it all to end, and now it had. The shell of that life was below them, in the valley, and their lives were up here.

Tosh, Peirce and I waited for Aphra. Where was she? I couldn't fathom why she'd run away. I also worried that in the rush of so many people something might have happened to her.

Peirce jarred me from my anxiety with his bark. I turned around and saw Aphra walking toward me beside her mother, Abe, and Paul. A lump appeared in my throat. I closed my eyes and let out a sigh. Peirce jumped up on Abe and Abe caught him. Then Peirce began to lick his face.

Aphra ran up and hugged me.

"Where have you been?" I asked.

"With Glen," she said calmly. "He had a lot to tell me."

I looked at Melinda. "He told us to wait for her at the top of the tunnel."

In the escape from the jail, Glen thought it best if Melinda, Paul and Abe separated from him, in case the police captured him. He showed them which tunnel to follow and was gone.

"He also wanted me to say to you thank you," Aphra added.

The fate of Glen Harding remained a secret. There were a few who claimed to have seen him on the mountain, but the accounts were contradictory. Only one person knew with certainty where he was, and she had learned to keep secrets.

*

For fifteen years after the orange incident, I wandered around the country, staying briefly in different places, taking different jobs. I couldn't settle down anywhere because Harding was always on my mind. It haunted me. I did try to visit it on several occasions, but the area remained closed to visitors. The State barricaded the roads, fenced off and paroled the area to keep the curious away. Their plan was to demolish the city.

In those years Aphra graduated from university with a dual degree in physics and environmental science, and now lived on her own in Virginia. Melinda, Paul and Abe lived in nearby Warren, Pennsylvania. Tosh and Peirce had passed away. Both were buried in the mountains around Harding.

Aphra and I remained in contact. We founded a group, the Harding Lobby, to convince the government to open Harding for tours. For years we pressured officials and kept the orange events in the news and on social media. We tried to constantly remind everyone of its importance. The authorities finally gave us permission to proceed, but insisted Harding remain out-of-the-way, off the main thoroughfare, and without any hotels or restaurants close by. The barricades and patrols would stay. No funds to finance the tours were available. There would be no effort to publicize or designate it as an historical site.

The Harding Lobby then began to fundraise and succeeded in finding private financing, with Lobby volunteers as guides and caretakers. We offered three commemorative tours each year: when the orange first appeared, when Glen climbed the pole, and when the prisons opened and the residents fled the city.

During those three days a year, the hut would become a visitor center. Tours would start at the hut and continue down the mountains through the paths. The group would walk the streets and imagine how the Harding residents dealt with the orange and see the square where they reported each day. Highlights would be the pole on which Glen stood high above the ground, the Sheffield statue chipped by bullets, and the factory prisons, where we hoped visitors could envision how the government and Guard restricted the residents.

Aphra and I texted and video-chatted often about Harding, excited by the day of the first tour, when the Guard and patrols lowered their barriers. On that day, before the first public tour, Aphra and I went alone with Aphra as the guide.

We first went to the gravesites of Tosh and Peirce and paid our respects. The sites were close to one of the places where the four of us had sat together and looked down upon Harding during the orange days. Aphra hugged the ground where Abe and she had buried Peirce. It was hard not to wish in some way those days could return. How dear they seem now, when we heard Tosh tell us of the events in Harding and watched Peirce chase after butterflies and squirrels.

We then hiked down the mountain, into the tunnels, and across the bridge to the city. Though covered with fifteen years of neglect, everything had survived: the jail, the factory prisons, the graffiti, the smashed windows and doors, the bridges, the City Café, the house where Abe, Paul and Peirce lived, the metal grasshoppers, the tunnels, and the original plaques. Only the orange was absent.

Then she led me to the small home of Glen Harding, slightly north of the city near the river, surrounded with firs. It was my first visit. Walking through its few rooms, laden with dust, I saw tables stacked with books on physics, math, science, magic, art, philosophy, and mysticism, and others laden with inventions and scientific instruments, the purpose of which has remained unclear. The house itself was spare and showed little care. Walls required paint. There were a few pieces of old and worn furniture. On the walls were many photographs of scenes and objects from odd vantage points.

"Each of these photographs," she said, "refers to one of Glen's schemes 'to restore nature,' as he put it."

"For example, this one's about the horse stealing. It doesn't show the horse, only a tiny section of the yard from where he took the horse."

Next she guided me into the basement where what appeared to be a wall of dirt hid an entrance to the tunnels. Then she brought me up to the second floor. At the top of the stairs, was a large photo of Aphra. In the bedroom closet was a hidden attic door that opened upon a circular iron stairway.

In the center was a model of the valley, mountains, the town, and tiny hand-made figurines of animals. Scattered about the papier-mâché terrain were little replicas of markers, each labeled with a Greek letter, and below each of them were miniature mirrors, prisms, amplifiers, and other unknown mechanisms invented by Glen, all of them directed to the pole in the square. As we stared at the model, an orange-colored light covered it.

"Do you know how all this works?" I asked.

She smiled.

"I helped him set it up. He created a powerful refractory effect through mirrors and prisms placed throughout the area, and magnification of orange light. The location of the orange light itself he never showed me, but I know that he combined several strong sources in several locations. I always assumed they were in the trees."

She led me back downstairs and out into the overgrown front yard where we enjoyed the sight of the mountains. While the city had fossilized, the land upon which it stood was becoming increasingly abundant.

"It's amazing, isn't it?" Aphra said. "The mountainsides are slowly filling in again with trees and wildflowers, the streams have more fish than ever and far fresher water; and the forest creatures are slowly retaking their homes. Even the wolf is returning. The forest is creeping in on the city itself."

"What of Glen?" I asked. My own theory was that he lived out his life in that same area, that he never left the valley where his family had first settled. I had a romantic notion that some future explorer might find his skull and bones in an underground cave, as well as his book that he was supposedly writing.

She shrugged.

If she knew the answer—and I think she did know it—she didn't share it with me that day.

"Come visit me in Redfield, Virginia next summer," Aphra said when we parted. "Park in the Appalachian Trail lot near Damascus and walk south to a path that leads up the mountains. Here's a map."

*

The next year I followed her instructions. After an hour of hiking I found the path and climbed until I stood on a high point encircled by the Blue Ridge Mountains, close to the border of Tennessee. As Aphra's map indicated, another path led down to Redfield. I was anxious to see her, but that was only part of the thrill. Looking down over the valley, my eyes were seduced by the bluish-purple haze that was cloaking the town.

THE END of

ORANGE DAWN

Author's Bio-Data

John Clark Smith grew up in Rochester, New York, U.S.A., but his heritage originates in western Pennsylvania, the setting for *Orange Dawn*. Prior to *Orange Dawn*, John's book, *Taking Action*, was published in September 2019. It is a collection of stories appearing in reviews and journals between 2016-2019.  Prior to 2016, when he began to submit his stories, plays and poetry, his graduate studies on the philosopher Charles Peirce, the ancient thinker Origen, and a translation from the ancient Greek and Latin were published as well as several scholarly articles. He is a graduate of Syracuse University, Duke University, the University of Toronto at St. Michael's College (Ph.D.), has a diploma from the Graduate Program in Creative Writing at Humber College, and an A.R.C.T. in music from the Royal Conservatory of Music. John has served as a Managing Director (England), Project Manager (China), Music Director (U.S.A.), and a University Lecturer on how the arts can transform us. John lives with his wife Susan and is the proud father of daughters Tammy and Amara, and son John.